The Cowboy's Secret Wish

THE COWBOY'S SECRET WISH

THE COWBOYS OF SWEETHEART CREEK, TEXAS
BOOK 2

JEAN ORAM

The Cowboy's Secret Wish

The Cowboys of Sweetheart Creek, Texas (Book 2)

By Jean Oram

© 2020 Jean Oram
All rights reserved
First Edition

This is a work of fiction and all characters, organizations, places, events, and incidents appearing in this novel are products of the author's active imagination or are used in a fictitious manner unless otherwise stated. Any resemblance to actual people, alive or dead, as well as any resemblance to events or locales is coincidental and, truly, a little bit cool. Unless you're the mayor of Sweetheart Creek, in which case you may bear a resemblance to someone whose name rhymes with Travis. But that's where reality ends. (Right, person-whose-name-actually-does-rhyme-with-Donna?)

Printed in the United States of America unless otherwise stated on the last page of this book. Published by Oram Productions Alberta, Canada.

COMPLETE LIBRARY OF CONGRESS CATALOGING-IN-PUBLICATION DATA AVAILABLE ONLINE

Oram, Jean.

The Cowboy's Secret Wish / Jean Oram.—1st. ed.

ISBN: 978-1-989359-30-3, 978-1-989359-31-0

Ebook ISBN: 978-1-989359-29-7

First Oram Productions Edition: November 2020

Cover design by Jean Oram

ACKNOWLEDGMENTS

A big thank you goes to Margaret Carney, Tessa Shapcott, Donna W, Margaret C, Sharon S., Erika H., and Sarah A., as well as my error finding team.

A NOTE FROM THE AUTHOR

As a writer you just never know when something from your life will find its way into a story.

Such as going on a county agricultural tour with friends and getting to talk to some avid beer brewers who are experimenting and having fun with their jobs by creating Lambic beers. This is definitely where I got the idea for Ryan's Lambic beer—I am pretty sure the real thing tastes better than Ryan's!

Or maybe it's a past job such as my time as a librarian. Although, the libraries I've worked in didn't end up with a dog like Karen did. But I still think it's a good idea. (And I do like the illustrated version of *The Da Vinci Code*. It's pretty cool, and the students thought so, too.)

Or it could even be moving out of my comfortable zone and joining the local ladies league despite not yet knowing the rules of golf, or really even which clubs to use when.

All of these things have somehow wound their way into what I think of as the sweetest couple's story from my The Cowboys of Sweetheart Creek, Texas series.

I hope you enjoy these slivers of real life woven into the pages of Myles and Karen's story.

Happy reading,
Jean Oram
Alberta, Canada 2020

To the Gull Lake Golf Course and the ladies from the 2019 league who taught me everything I know about golf and allowed me to play on their teams while I figured out the game. And as for that time I managed to reach par before I even left the tee box... I thank my team for their enduring kindness and patience.

———————

*M*yles Wylder sat on a square hay bale outside the old converted barn, country music filtering out into the cool Texas October night. Another family rolled up in their four-door pickup, ready to dance and raise some funds for Alexa McTavish's local horse sanctuary set outside of Sweetheart Creek. Myles stood and shifted the donation jar on the nearby table so its label faced the approaching group.

Glancing over his shoulder, he watched family and friends through the barn's open doors. His gaze connected with the bright eyes of Karen Hartley, the local librarian, and he quickly looked away. She hadn't danced all night. And so far, neither had he.

Just like at last weekend's community barn dance.

"Hey, Myles. Looking sharp tonight." It was Mayor Travis Nestner, his wife, Donna, and their triplet daughters. "The boys are looking promising out on the field. This the year you win State?"

"We'll see. The boys have a lot of potential." Myles had been coaching the high school's football team with his younger brother, Ryan, for several years, and they'd narrowly missed winning their division's state championship as many times.

"I enjoyed watching you play all those years ago." The mayor had been a few classes ahead, and played football himself. He'd even caught the attention of a few college scouts, but a shoulder injury late in his senior year had knocked him out of contention.

"Yeah, I still miss it," Myles said. He'd been the team's enforcer. The brute. The heavy. The protector. The brick wall. And somehow that had become his full-time identity even years after he'd left the field as a player.

Myles glanced into the dance hall again. Even in her Western wear, Karen looked like the intellectual she was. Maybe it was the glasses, or the simple white blouse absent of fringe, its subtle pattern designed to blend in. She was laughing at something Jackie Moorhouse had said, and her head was tipped back, her long white throat exposed. He wondered what had made her laugh so openly and with such abandon. Around him she acted reserved, guarded, and almost as though she expected him to pick her up and carry her off somewhere.

Maybe she had special talents as a mind reader.

Travis shoved some bills into the donation jar. "For the horses."

"Thanks."

"We get to dance again this weekend!" one of the girls said to Myles. She clicked her small cowboy boots together and lifted her pink cowboy hat as if about to break into a dance routine.

"I know, right?" he said. "How'd we get so lucky to have an extra barn dance this month?" The girls beamed and Myles asked Donna, who was carrying a white casserole dish for the potluck supper, "Are those your famous hot wings?"

"My secret recipe. Fresh from the frozen food aisle and hot from the oven."

"Save me a few."

"I'll do you one better and bring you a plate."

"Thanks."

The Nestners went inside the barn, the girls racing onto the floor to join their friends in a line dance.

Myles turned to find Wade Ross standing in front of him, grinning like he'd fallen too far into the whiskey again.

"This is a dry event, Wade."

"Hey, it's me!" He laughed, pretending to throw punches at Myles's gut. Myles watched, unamused. The man didn't seem to comprehend that Myles could flatten him with one quick left hook should he try.

"Seriously. It's a dry event."

Wade lifted his hands, his tone exasperated. "I know, I know. You tell me that every time."

"And they call *me* the slow learner. I hope someone gave you a ride."

"I walked." The man hiccuped.

Myles surveyed the grassy area where people parked behind the barn, which was located a few miles from Sweetheart Creek. He didn't see Wade's blue pickup. He took a few steps farther from his post to look around the corner of the barn. In the distance, near the road, a green tractor was parked at an angle in the ditch.

"Driving your tractor while under the influence is still drinking and driving."

"I walked!" The man staggered two steps, then spun around and swung, his right fist missing Myles's nose but knocking his black cowboy hat into the dirt. Myles dodged as he swung again, then widened his stance, ready to protect himself in case Wade was one drink beyond making wise decisions.

Behind Wade, Donna was exiting the barn, her attention on calling out a hello to someone still inside while she brought Myles his promised plate of wings.

Wade swung again, coming close enough to knocking into

Donna that Myles grabbed his arm and twisted it behind his back. "That's enough. Ladies are present."

The mayor's wife came to a halt, realizing she'd almost been hit.

"I was just playing around. Don't be so dumb." Wade yanked his arm free of Myles's loose grip.

Myles clenched his hands. "Speak for yourself."

"Wade Ross! You nearly made me drop my wings," Donna drawled, with a look of disdain. She handed the plate to Myles and flashed him a smile. "Enjoy, honey."

As she headed back inside, Wade muttered, "I hope your high school football career was worth the cash you paid me to tutor you in English, because I sure enjoyed buying that Chevy Charger with your hard-earned money."

Myles let out a slow breath to calm himself. He would never have allowed his coach to set him up with Wade as his tutor if he'd known how often the man would find a way to throw it in his face.

"And I can see *your* high grades set you up for the good life," Myles said, keeping his cool when Wade made a fake lunge at him, then turned to enter the dance with a scowl.

Myles bent to retrieve his hat, wondering how good hitting Wade would feel, and if it would be worth it. Ryan, inside the dance hall, wandered past the entrance and Myles tipped his head toward Wade, receiving a nod from his brother. Ryan would keep an eye on him, and if this Saturday night was like most others, Myles would end up driving a barely conscious Wade home around ten.

Maybe a smarter man would call the sheriff to take care of the drunk man, not look out for him each time the community held a barn dance. But at the same time, Myles understood that having your wife leave you the same month you lost your family's eighty-year-old business due to changes in the global economy had a way of turning someone upside down.

4

Myles sat on his bale again as more vehicles turned off the dirt road and into the grassy parking area. Unable to help himself, he turned to glance inside the barn once more, catching Karen watching him with a look that made him cringe. She'd made it clear she wasn't into men displaying how much testosterone they had, and jousting with Wade had likely earned him that frown.

Myles sighed and focused on savoring his wings while welcoming the newcomers, thanking them as they made donations or added a scoop of whatever they were taking to the potluck onto his plate. He really didn't know why so few people volunteered to work the door. You got to see everyone and you got first dibs on most of the food, too.

"Hi, Myles." A sticky-sweet female voice made him cringe.

Uh-oh. Here was one more reason for Karen to frown at him: Daisy-Mae Ray. The woman had made a career of fawning over him, and until recently he'd never minded one bit. He turned to the bleached blonde sashaying toward him in sparkly cowboy boots. Her hair was as large as her ego and her denim shirt so short she probably couldn't lift her arms without revealing something round.

She was his type. Or at least had been for a very long time.

But as Myles approached his thirtieth year he found himself looking for more in terms of conversation, and he knew from experience it wouldn't come from Daisy-Mae. She wasn't slow-witted, but she wasn't interested in changing her world, other than possibly adding a husband to the mix.

She sat beside him on the hay bale, her hand landing on his thigh with a firm squeeze that made him tense. Angling close, she ran a finger down the front of the light sweater he was wearing under a blazer.

"Did you just come from a funeral?" Daisy-Mae leaned her chest against him as though ready to provide comfort should he say the word.

"No."

He had chosen something a bit dressier tonight because apparently he was into being obvious. Normally he wore a Sweetheart Creek Torpedoes football jersey, or a T-shirt that showed off his muscles. Or if he was feeling particularly dressy, a Western shirt. But never a blazer.

Daisy-Mae was petting him now and he gently extracted her hands, clasping them between his own. "I'm okay. Really."

"I've been lonely lately," she said, those glossy pink lips of hers pouting in an open invitation to kiss them, to get lost in her for a while.

"You know, Brant is single." He might as well throw his middle brother under the bus. He liked to play rescue hero for the women around town, stepping in as a fake boyfriend whenever they needed one to ward off suitors. Daisy-Mae didn't need to ward anyone off at the moment, but Myles did.

"We used to have fun times, you and me." Her fingers were tangling in the neckline of his sweater, stretching it. He felt she might be one second from ripping it over his head. "What went wrong?"

He scooted away, then stood. "We did have fun. You know, Brant thinks you're hot." Which was true. Pretty much every man in town found Daisy-Mae attractive on some level.

"That's adorable."

"But?"

"I took my princess, Ella, to him the other day because she was acting funny, and he said she was just fine."

"Maybe she was?"

Brant was down-to-earth and empathetic, and his career as the town veterinarian worked like an ever-present wingman in the dating arena. Women took their pets to him for the strangest reasons in hopes of landing a date or an engagement ring. So far everyone seemed to be striking out.

"Will you dance with me tonight?" Daisy-Mae batted her

lashes, giving him a helpless, innocent look that used to work on him like a charm.

"Sorry, I'm stuck on the door shift." He gestured to the donation jar. "For the horses."

She turned toward the open barn. Inside, the dance floor was filling up, lit by bare bulbs hanging on strings above, while the tables along the edges were crowded by people enjoying the community potluck. Ryan was walking by again, and Daisy-Mae hustled forward, snagging his sleeve and pulling him out the door.

"Ryan, honey, we have a problem."

"What's that?" he asked, looking distracted. He took a sip from his bottle of root beer.

"I need to dance with Myles, but he has to watch the door."

Behind her, Myles shook his head and dragged a finger across his throat.

"I would be happy to solve that problem for you, Daisy-Mae," Ryan said all too graciously. "Let me take over so Myles can spin you around the dance floor for as long as y'all would like."

Daisy-Mae wiggled with happiness and, beaming, took Myles by the hand and hauled him into the barn.

"I owe you one," Myles said over his shoulder, his tone flat and emotionless.

"Enjoy yourself," his brother called back, settling onto the hay bale with a self-satisfied grin before finishing off Myles's last hot wing.

On the dance floor Myles held out his arms and sucked in a deep breath as Daisy-Mae skittered closer. Her skimpy outfit meant he was either going to have to put his palm on some of her exposed skin or a little too low on her denim skirt to be polite.

Why did country dancing involve having the man's hand on a woman's waist, anyway? Because when it came right down to it, there was only one woman he wanted to have his hands on, and he was pretty sure, judging from the way the librarian had just turned her back, that she wanted nothing to do with him.

KAREN HARTLEY FOUND her gaze drawn toward Myles Wylder as he twirled Daisy-Mae Ray on the dance floor, spinning her out in a swift, sharp move that nearly left the woman stumbling. She frowned. Something was up. Myles was a better dancer than that. And what was with the fitted sweater and blazer tonight?

Myles pulled Daisy-Mae back in again, and she tumbled against his broad chest, beaming up at him. Karen turned away in disgust. The woman was so obvious. Didn't that bother him?

Karen tried to focus on something else in the barn, but found herself catching sight of a small cluster of women she often noticed at the Torpedoes football games. They were smiling at Myles from the edge of the dance floor, sending him little waves whenever he glanced their way. Just like when he was coaching, he was polite, giving a tip of his hat, a nod, a smile, or a quiet hello. Watching him be fawned over always left Karen feeling drab, plain and about as sexy as a cardboard box.

Unable to help herself, she peeked again at Daisy-Mae, who was currently pressed tight to Myles's body as they moved across the floor. What would it feel like to have a strong man hold you with such assurance, his large hand cupping yours? The warmth of his palm on your waist? The promise of his virility and passion on a level where there was no thinking, no contemplating, just acting on instinct?

"Karen? Hello?" Jackie Moorhouse was waving a hand in front of Karen's face. She was wearing a sympathetic, yet under-standing smile. "Sorry to say it, honey, but you're the furthest thing from his type."

Karen snapped into focus, dropping her hold on the antique gold chain she was wearing. "Whose type?"

"I saw you visually undressing Myles Wylder."

Oh no. Now she was imagining what that would be like. All that muscle and bare skin. So unlike her past boyfriends, whose only overdeveloped parts tended to be their brains. And why, whenever she was around Myles, did she have to remind herself she was looking for brains, not brawn?

"You have a thing for him in a blazer?" Jackie asked.

"Was he at a funeral?" Karen hurt at the thought of him being in pain.

"I don't think so."

Her gaze drifted toward the broad-shouldered man once again. When he wore his typical jersey, jeans and plain brown cowboy boots she thought he was sexy, that casual, confident air about him always catching her attention. But tonight in those black boots, dark wash jeans that fitted as though the designer had had him in mind... The thin sweater that hugged his pecs before clinging to his tight abdomen, and the blazer overtop, which made him look as though he was...

Words failed her. Not even a thesaurus could help her tonight, because there were no adjectives in the English language for a man who looked as delectably perfect as he did. Sexy didn't even begin to cover it. With that black hat he looked like every fantasy, the kind of guy who could shake your world with one hot, smoldering look.

She shook her head, clearing away the unexpected haze of lust that had come over her.

"He looks very handsome tonight," Karen said primly, smoothing her white blouse against her ribs. "He is also everything I am *not* looking for in a man." She gave Jackie a serious glance over the tops of her glasses. She felt her cheeks heating up, but didn't quite understand why. The men she dated were PhD candidates, book nerds, and the type that listened to NPR and discussed current issues at length over espressos. She wanted a man who challenged her and her assumptions, who preferred to use his brain, not his fists. She wanted someone who was constantly learning and growing, curious about the world—not looking to settle down with the first pretty thing to happen along. And even more, she wanted one who didn't wrestle with other adult men as if he was still on the football field.

Myles Wylder was a cowboy, ex-football-player, and coach who was currently allowing Miss Sweet Hills County to stroke her fingers over his chest.

Karen turned away in disgust. Why did she keep watching them?

"I caught him looking at you earlier," Jackie whispered.

A ripple of chills ran down Karen's spine. She breathed out slowly, saying calmly, "Probably because he saw me staring at him, trying to figure out what was different about him tonight."

"And?"

"He got a haircut."

Jackie laughed. "A haircut? He is the sexiest cowboy in the entire barn. He has women drooling over him, he's wearing something completely out of character, and you notice his hair?"

Her friend shook her head with a knowing smile that made Karen want to hide for the rest of the night.

"It's not as shaggy around his collar."

"You have it bad, sweetheart. Bad. But I get it. If Myles asked me to spend the night with him, I wouldn't say no."

That thought sobered her up. She'd known since her first day in town almost eight years ago that the Wylders were off-limits. Jackie Moorhouse wanted a Wylder, and she would get one. Karen valued Jackie's friendship way more than some ill-thought-out *anything* with Man-Candy Myles.

Their friend April MacFarlane joined them, balancing three plastic cups of sweet tea. Motherhood had rounded out her figure, something she fussed about, saying she wished she could lose the fifty pounds she'd gained, but Karen envied how voluptuous she had become. The woman had some serious va-voom going on.

"Jackie, honey, Karen wants Myles, so give him up." April handed out the sweet tea.

"I—I don't," Karen sputtered.

April's four-year-old son, Kurt, stood beside his mom, adorable in his cowboy boots and hat. He was holding a half glass of sweet tea and looking very serious with his crystalline blue eyes and wavy brown hair. He looked like April and Heath, but could also pass for Myles's nephew.

"Karen is in what's called denial." Jackie turned to the little boy. "Right, Kurt?"

He nodded soberly, his bright eyes focused on her.

"But enough about the Wylders," Jackie said, surprising Karen. She turned to April, asking pointedly, "How are things?"

April had recently confessed she was considering pulling the cord on her marriage to Heath Thompson, a former rodeo star and now rodeo stock contractor. She said if she did, it would be in one sharp, quick move, and she'd sworn them to secrecy.

However, the couple had arrived at last week's barn dance looking happy. They'd laughed and danced, seeming like a perfect little family. Tonight, though, April was alone again, the dark shadows under her eyes having returned.

"We had a long, honest chat and last week was pretty good." April glanced down at her son before carefully saying, "But it didn't last, and I can't keep arguing about what I need every single week like it's something new to him."

Jackie gave April's arm a supportive squeeze.

"Hey, look what I found," Brant Wylder said, coming up with a tabby kitten.

"A cat!" Kurt grinned and lurched forward, almost spilling his drink in the process.

Karen reached over and quickly righted the plastic cup.

"Can we go play with it while you gals chat?" Brant asked.

April nodded. As he left with the small child, Jackie's gaze followed him.

"Brant's pretty sweet," Karen said.

"He's amazing," April stated.

"I heard he bought someone a house," Jackie whispered, and Karen instinctively leaned in to hear the latest on the house mystery.

Jackie looked to April in question and she replied firmly, "He's the best *friend* a gal could ask for."

"And maybe a little bit more?" Jackie hinted.

"I'm *married*."

"Why don't you finally snag him?" Karen asked Jackie.

"I have a feeling someone might be holding out for Cole," April said slyly.

"Enough about the Wylders," Jackie said for the second time that night, making Karen wonder what was going on. She was always happy to talk about the five brothers and how she was crushing on all of them. Well, just the four now, seeing as Levi had recently found true love with fashion model Laura Oakes.

The band playing in the corner of the barn picked up its tempo and a couple came spinning by, nearly crashing into the trio of friends. The woman was beaming at her dance partner in a way that made Karen wish she could find someone who would cause her to light up like that.

Not that any of her relationships had been bad, and she was sure there had been love in at least one or two, but there hadn't been that spark that lit up everything from the inside out. And the older she got, the more she longed to see if that was something that could happen to her.

"How are things at the library?" April asked. "Sorry we didn't make it to story hour last week."

"It's totally drop-in," Karen said, taking a sip of her sweet tea.

"How did the last budget meeting go?" Jackie asked.

"Not too well." The library was in trouble and the recent cuts across town had put her job at risk. Her hours were sure to be cut to almost nothing by year's end.

Currently, Karen worked three days a week at the town library, with the occasional Saturday thrown in, alongside two other part-timers and several volunteers. On Fridays she filled in at the elementary school library, and on Monday and Wednesday evenings she tutored high school students—all in hopes of meeting her financial goals of retiring sometime before the age of ninety-nine. If she lost her job at the town library, she wasn't sure what she'd do. She couldn't see herself serving tables at The Longhorn Diner, drinks at The Watering Hole, or Jenny Oliver needing her to help sell cowboy boots at Blue Tumbleweed. Those were the top three local employers for anyone in her weight class, seeing as she wasn't strong enough to wrangle cattle.

"Are you going to put on a fundraiser?" Jackie asked, referring to the idea Myles had come up with a few days ago, while helping Karen carry a box of books. She'd told the girls about it, still dazzled by his sudden appearance, his help with the heavy box and the way she'd felt when he'd looked at her as if he'd wanted to kiss her. Her friends had thought his idea was brilliant.

Raising money was a good idea, but working with Myles? How could they—two opposites—possibly make a good team? They'd have completely different viewpoints on everything, and she was fairly certain he'd drive her to drink—or distraction.

"I can help," Jackie said. "Just say the word."

April nodded, agreeing.

"It was just an idea," Karen said, focusing on her sweet tea.

"An idea from Myles," Jackie pointed out, "and you're afraid what working together might lead to." Her tone turned more serious as she added, "You know he's on my list, but if he makes you an offer, you go for it. He's a catch and you're a good friend." She winked and gave a nonchalant shrug. "I'm willing to cut a Wylder loose for a friend like you."

Karen almost choked in surprise. "It will never be that kind of offer."

"So then? What's the holdup? Why not work with Myles?"

"It'd take a lot of effort to raise that much money. If we took on the project I might as well put my résumé online now." She gave a sharp nod, feeling the truth of her words. "We couldn't save the library together if our lives depended upon it."

MYLES MANAGED to extract himself from Daisy-Mae after several dances and found himself standing in front of Karen Hartley. She looked at him with her large dark eyes as though waiting for something. Wordlessly, he held out his hand.

She hesitated a beat, received a none-too-subtle nudge from her friend Jackie, then placed her small, cool hand in his. It was at that moment he realized he was going to be reckless. He knew nothing about literature, and as further proof of their differences she had shot down his suggestion to work together to save the library. And if he really needed to feel bad about himself and think about how different they were, he simply had to remember the time in early September after a football game when he had been goofing around with his brothers, April and Jackie out on the field. They'd been tossing the football, laughing and yelling, chasing each other down. Uncharacteristically, Karen had appeared on the sidelines wearing a sweatshirt—one that sported the team's name—with that look he'd noticed she often got when watching the game or the cheerleaders. It was half cool assessment and half longing. He had immediately recognized her feeling of being excluded, and without thinking, he'd sent her the ball, putting a perfect spiral on his pass. But she hadn't moved into position to receive it, and in a panic, he'd called out her name just as the pass angled downward and she'd looked up, getting clocked in the nose.

He'd been mortified when she'd stumbled backward, landing on her butt. She'd recovered quickly, sprinting off the field, clutching her bloody nose. While Myles had stood frozen in shock, Jackie had hurried after her with a dirty look and a "Really, Myles?"

He was pretty sure Karen had never forgiven him for that. Not even after he'd heard Rhonda, the cheer coach, moaning about organization and how she needed a manager, and he'd mentioned the librarian's many skills. Karen had taken to the managerial role like a fish to water. But he still felt as though there was something unresolved between them, and that he had something to make up for.

The band changed songs, moving to a slow one just as Myles placed his hand on Karen's waist to lead her into the throng of dancers. She froze as the tempo changed, as though unsure how to proceed.

He knew how.

He placed his left foot just outside her right one, then curved his hand around her slender waist, allowing his fingers to slide almost to the small of her back as he moved into dance position. Her free hand was light on his shoulder, as though she feared touching him.

And yet there was something in the way she looked at him combined with how he felt around her that seemed like a recipe for recklessness. He wanted to travel down her road to see what was at the end, even though he was certain there would be a fatal crash somewhere along the way.

He was taller than she was by at least eight inches and he crooked his neck to check her expression. "Ready?"

She straightened her spine in that defiant way he'd seen her do only around him. "I was born ready."

He quelled the urge to smile and gave a brief nod as he moved her onto the floor, adoring her moxie. There was more to her than the serious librarian persona she touted like a badge, but he sensed that in order to find the real Karen, he was going to have to play along until she was ready to drop her outer shield.

"Read any good books lately?" he asked, moving slowly from foot to foot.

"Seriously?" Her eyes twinkled with amusement, and her tone was one of disbelief. She was a smooth dancer despite her apparent discomfort with how he'd moved in close. He had expected this to become an awkward, stumbling dance, but she was surprisingly comfortable to dance with.

"So you've read more than one good book lately?"

She rolled her eyes and he tamped down his urge to laugh. She looked so disgruntled by his attempt at conversation.

"Let's move along to your next pickup line," she said, and he wondered if her sass was a form of self-preservation. "Are you going to ask if I'm a library book, because you'd like to check me out?"

This time he didn't hide his mirth, but allowed laughter to vibrate through him. "Too late. I've already checked you out." When he smiled down at her, her cheeks flushed pink, and then redder.

She lifted the hand that had been hovering lightly on his shoulder and gave him a sharp but painless smack. "Myles Wylder, you are officially a brat."

"I'm glad you finally noticed."

"Oh, I noticed a long time ago. I just don't find your brattiness as charming as you think I should."

"I see," he said slowly, determining his next approach. She was endearingly flustered, her sass quite possibly flirtatious, and after this amount of arguing with a woman he'd usually be kissing her. He had a feeling people didn't tease or banter with Karen very often, which was a shame as she was quick-witted, with a tongue that was sharp yet gentle.

"Have *you* read any good books lately?" She gave him a sweet smile.

The question felt like a barb and he debated not replying.

"I'm reading a book right now," he said cautiously, half expecting her to laugh.

"Really? And when did you start it?"

"Is that important?" he asked in confusion. Her tongue *was* sharp, and maybe not as gentle as he'd assumed.

"So the book you're reading is sitting on your bedside table collecting dust, and has been for several years?" Her tone was knowing, slightly haughty, as though she expected she was catching him in a fib.

"It's a book on coaching football. And I started it a few weeks ago." It was busting his chops, but she didn't need to know that.

"Hmm. Football?" She seemed to think that over for a second before dismissing it.

"That's right. Football." He wanted to tell her about his online courses, and how he was upgrading his skills in hopes of increasing his pay as a coach, so he would be less financially dependent on the ranch and its income. But he kept his mouth shut.

She wasn't focusing on him any longer, and he searched for something that might show her they weren't as different as she thought—even though they probably were even more so.

"I also enjoyed *The Da Vinci Code*." Well, he had found it interesting when his brother Ryan, a teacher, had talked about it. Ryan had spent an entire two-hour bus ride to a football game going on about various aspects of history touched upon in the book, and how his students had enjoyed finding hidden clues within the text and referenced artwork.

"It was a very popular book."

"You didn't like it?"

"It had its charm."

"Unlike me?"

"You have yours as well." She gave him a smile that had a hint of wickedness.

They continued to dance while he savored the idea of her thinking he had charm. As soon as he figured out which part she liked, he'd bring it out to play more often.

"I'm not embarrassed that I enjoyed the way the author pulled old art into the book," he said, deciding Karen might be a verified book snob, and the only way to get her to notice him would be to play along.

"You liked that?" She was considering him now, her dark eyes taking him in, and he felt emboldened.

"So what if not everyone enjoys the author's writing style? It got a lot of people reading. Isn't that the purpose of books?"

She made a pensive humming sound, her lips pressed into a fine line. Her eyes glittered with approval and he could feel himself reaching, searching for more ways to extend that acceptance. "You're not the mindless football player everyone makes you out to be."

She definitely wasn't as gentle as he'd thought.

"Is that why you don't want my help saving the library?" he said finally, fearing it was the truth.

She inhaled sharply, stiffening in his arms.

"You fear I'll be too slow to keep up with you, or to be of any help." He'd stopped moving, and her gaze had dropped, no longer darting to snag his.

He removed his hands from where he'd been cradling her warm body. "I guess if you don't care enough about our community to try and save a program that matters, then that's your prerogative and none of my business."

He tipped his hat, his heart hard and full of hurt. "Good night, Ms. Hartley. See you around."

2

_K_aren had really stepped in it with Myles last night. She had seen it the moment she'd referred to him as a mindless football player, and then had been too mortified by his expression and response to defend herself. She'd become tongue-tied, waiting for the verbal lashing she so richly deserved.

He was not brainless; she knew that from watching him coach his team out on the football field. It was clear he understood his players' strengths and weaknesses as well as those of their opponents. She should know. Being on the sidelines with the cheer squad she received exclusive insight into what the coaches were saying and doing. She had grabbed at the insult as though it could shield her against how good it felt to be in his arms, and she had blurted out the hurtful words without considering the man she'd aimed them at.

When she'd gone home from the dance, noting that Myles had left earlier than usual, she had headed to her bookshelf, finding an old gift from a teacher to use as a peace offering—assuming she didn't chicken out after Tuesday night's practice and fail to give it to Myles. As insurance against future excuses for not making the gesture, she'd put the book in her car's backseat pocket so it would be handy wherever she went.

As she swung her car toward Jackie's house, Karen took a detour past the high school to see if Myles's truck was parked there, his familiar form jogging around the track like he often did on Sunday mornings. Today the lot was empty, the track looking as dusty and dry as usual for mid-October.

Feeling disappointed as well as relieved, Karen pulled up at Jackie's, where her friend chucked her golf clubs in the backseat with a clatter, knowing Karen's were hogging the trunk. Karen had been cajoled into joining the Texas Meadows Golf and Country Club mixed league, thirty miles from Sweetheart Creek, as part of her friend's stay-fit-and-meet-a-man plan.

Jackie threw herself into the passenger seat, looking slightly out of place in her golf garb instead of her usual Western wear.

"Why did we choose golf again?" Jackie asked, as she tugged at her cute golf skirt.

"Because I'm not athletic and you promised me a lack of coordination wouldn't matter."

As she said it, Karen felt her lips twist into a frown. She'd basically been reliving her worst high school gym class fears each time she stepped on the green. Every week, teamed up with someone new, she'd preemptively apologize, trying to make light of the fact that her performance would keep them out of that day's winners' circle. So far, though, nobody had mocked her with quite the same finesse and expertise as Duncan Small had in high school gym class.

One year she'd gone so far as to fake a myriad of injuries as a way to avoid the daily reminder of all her shortcomings, satisfying the teacher—who claimed she needed to do something gym-like—by reading up on various sports, her nose happily in a book each fourth period of the day. Naturally, Duncan had managed to "accidentally" hit her book with a basketball, dodge ball, badminton birdie, volleyball or soccer ball during class.

"You forgot a reason!" Jackie said brightly. "You're not marrying a cowboy, and cowboys don't play golf. Aka, it's a good way to meet the right kind of men."

Karen laughed. "Yeah, too bad Texas Meadows is nothing but a bunch of cowboys swinging sticks." The hypothesis that they'd meet a bunch of CEOs had been a dud.

"Maybe next year we can try tennis. Their skirts are shorter. And are you sure about adhering to your no-cowboy-boyfriends rule? There are some pretty nice cowboys around."

"Not my type."

"You mean you might as well reject them before they reject you, because they're not nerds and you only want a nerd?"

Karen let out a huff of air to express her disagreement.

"Maybe it's not the kind of man you need to focus on, but sending out the right vibes."

"What?"

"You know, undo a couple of buttons on your blouse. Show them you're available." Jackie laughed. "Quit frowning."

Karen sighed and put on her turn signal as she steered her Honda onto the highway through town. Jackie was likely right on more levels than Karen wanted to admit.

"I've gotten better," she muttered.

"That's true," her friend mused. "You do leave the top button open sometimes. You vixen." She gave a playful growl and swiped at the air as though she had claws, making Karen laugh and nearly strike an armadillo ambling across the pavement. She hit the brakes, allowing the animal to pause, hiss at her, then safely waddle off the road as though insulted.

"Seriously, that thing has a death wish," she muttered.

"You know what kind of animal Bill is?" Jackie asked, referring to the well-known local armadillo she'd just about hit.

"A mammal."

"He's a military-grade possum."

Karen gave an amused snort. "You're ridiculous."

"Save that one as a conversation starter. It makes men laugh, and it'll help overcome…this." She waved a hand at Karen's outfit.

"Hey! I am not all prim librarian today." She looked cute. Her Nike shorts were fitted, her golf shirt brought out the dark blue in her eyes and, she felt, also showed off her physique. "And what does it matter? I don't go for jocks or cowboys, and that's all that show up for league."

"Honey, you ironed your shorts."

"The club has a very strict dress code."

"Your top button is done up."

Karen fingered the neckline of her shirt. "So?" The idea of doing something against the rules and getting called on it was mortifying. If you couldn't play the game well, you might at least look as though you belonged.

Jackie had shifted so she was leaning against the passenger door, her focus solely on Karen.

"What?" Karen asked.

"Nothing."

"*What?*"

"I'm trying to figure out what you've got going on here that makes Myles drool over you like a prime cut of steak." She gave a playful wink and Karen felt her face flush with heat.

"He does not."

"Aw, you're blushing! That's so cute. Imagine what would happen if you undid a button. Or two. Or even *three*."

Karen rolled her eyes. Jackie was a good friend and always knew what to say, but she was off base with the whole Myles-drooling idea.

By the time they reached the golf course, the two friends were laughing, Karen's worries long forgotten.

As they drove through the gates of the country club, Jackie said, "If you want a nice man, come to a football game with me."

"I don't think so." Her friend had a reputation for hooking up friends with the love of their life at football games. Laura Oakes being the latest, although many argued that it hadn't actually been Jackie's doing. However, the first time Laura and Levi had kissed had been after the game Jackie had taken her to, so most people said it counted.

"I'm always down on the field managing the squad," Karen added.

"How much do cheerleaders even need once they're at the game? And just so you know, there are men on the sidelines, sweetie." Jackie grinned and climbed out of the car after Karen parked.

"None that are my type."

"Ryan is pretty brainy."

"He's so aloof he could give a cat pointers." Well, he wasn't quite that bad, but he was definitely a lone wolf and not the type to light her fire the way his brother Myles seemed to.

And why did her mind keep traveling back to Myles Wylder? He was wrong for her on every level.

Karen clapped her hands as though trying to scatter her thoughts. "Let's go find some hot men who know their way around a boardroom, and live happily ever after."

"Find men who know their way around a *bedroom?*" Jackie grinned. "I like the way you think, girl."

They began walking across the paved lot with their clubs, Karen shaking her head. "You're nothing but trouble."

"If that's what you need, I can find some before the day is through."

MYLES ROUNDED the corner of the Texas Meadows clubhouse, his golf bag slung over his shoulder. He was looking forward to whacking a few balls along the fairways to work out his frustrations.

So far this year he'd been unable to get out on the links during league, with the family ranch and coaching keeping him so busy. But Levi and Laura had just returned from New York, so Myles figured today was a perfect time to go golfing. His older brother, back from his first off-ranch holiday in forever, had launched into his usual take-charge role, double-checking everything that had or had not been done during his absence.

Myles had smiled, then performed his well-practiced vanishing act, setting his phone on Silent. It was time to reacquaint himself with his golf buddies, have a leisurely beer and spend a little time doing something he enjoyed. He leaned his clubs against the outdoor rack, then headed to the clubhouse entrance to check in, nearly running into a woman coming out. Myles stepped back to grab the door before realizing who it was. His heart scrambled as he battled anger and attraction.

Karen had left her hair down, her glossy black locks flowing neatly over her shoulders, a lovely lavender visor pulled down so far it nearly connected with her dark-rimmed glasses. She looked crisp and neat in her golf shorts and her collared shirt, which was buttoned up as far as it could go.

"Myles? Where's your cowboy hat?"

"I'm golfing," he said mildly. And based on her wardrobe, she was, too. Go figure she'd choose a sport that was about rules and decorum.

"You golf?" She appeared dumbfounded. Then she shook her head, eyebrows raised. "Of course you do."

Myles stared at her, unsure why she was acting so oddly. Maybe she felt remorse for her comments at last night's dance. That would be satisfying.

"Well, have a good game," she said, smoothing her shirt over her ribs, emphasizing her curves. "Mixed league is starting in a few minutes so you'd better get moving if you plan to hit the links."

"I'm in the league." He went to move past her, but she stopped him.

"I haven't seen you all season."

"Today's the first time I could make it." He eyed her skeptically. "I'm sure it'll be a blast."

"Well, make certain you pay your league fees. I don't want you winning a prize you haven't chipped in for." Her laugh wasn't the rich one he'd come to anticipate. This one was strained.

"Just hope you're on my team if you want a chance at that prize." He pushed past her, not caring when he jostled her shoulder with his chest.

That woman was a piece of work, and her new snobby attitude was getting under his skin. It didn't help that she was so agonizingly attractive. She thought she was above and beyond everything he did and everything he was.

And maybe she was right. He coached boys on how to crash into each other, whereas she coordinated the details for a team of girls who tumbled through the air with agility and grace.

Myles checked in at the desk, paid his league fees, then found a few old friends. They had some laughs while he sipped a beer that tasted a lot better than his brother Ryan's latest homemade batch, before heading out front to loosen up his swing on the practice putting green.

He was about to make a putt, a long one he was sure he'd lined up perfectly, when Karen Hartley came up beside him, surprising him. He tapped the ball too hard and it went bouncing off the green and into the rough.

"I wanted to apologize," she said. She was clutching her putter with white-knuckled fingers. She didn't seem to have a ball on her.

"For what?" he asked, trying not to sound impatient.

"What I said last night was unkind. It wasn't fair or right of me."

"But it's true?" He met her eyes, resting his putter on his foot. She didn't look away, her small chin almost quivering as she struggled to choose her next words, no doubt afraid he would stalk off before she could say whatever she'd rehearsed to make herself feel better again.

"I don't think so." She quickly shook her head, adjusting her glasses and knocking her visor off-kilter in the process. "I mean, the part about you not being dumb. That was true. I mean false. I mean…" She sucked in a big breath, her gaze caught on his sleeve where it snugged tightly over his biceps. He'd been meaning to buy a new shirt, but hadn't yet, and tried to subtly stretch the fabric a little lower. "I don't think you're a dumb jock." Her face was red, her expression mortified yet sincere as Myles inhaled slowly through his nose.

She stood there, putter clenched, her breath held. If she didn't look so frightened he'd have stalked away.

Plus it wasn't often people apologized for assuming or implying he was a dumb jock. He wasn't entirely sure what the protocol was.

He dropped a ball from his pocket and lined up his next putt. Then looked up when he heard his name being called.

"Let's hope you have a good team today, Wylder!" yelled a golfing friend, his tone amicable. "Because otherwise I'm going to mop the greens with y'all."

Karen's shoulders stiffened in response, her sweet, clean scent of soap wafting over him.

"Yeah, yeah," Myles said, ignoring her. "You say that every time, and every time I beat your score. He waved away the man's smack talk, receiving a laugh in return, and then focused on his putting again.

Karen started to walk away, then stopped, saying quietly so only he could hear, "And I do care about the library. I was surprised that you, a cowboy who never comes in, cares about it as much as you seem to."

He tapped the ball and it hit the hole's back rim and bounced away. Too much weight. He made a point of not glancing up at her while she tried to find the right words to complete her sentence. He had a feeling that if he looked into her eyes and saw that hesitant need to be seen, that one always simmering under the surface, that she could ask anything of him, say anything, then apologize, and all would be well in his world. Which was fine. Except he really didn't want to be a sucker.

He dropped another ball on the carpet of green below him.

"I would like to prevent the library from being shut down," she said slowly. "But I don't know how. I'm afraid that..."

For the first time since he'd met her, her confidence seemed to fail, her usual protective edge gone. Myles closed his eyes for a second, knowing he was doomed before he even looked up. "Afraid of failing?" he hazarded.

She bit her bottom lip, leaving a luscious dent in the pink flesh as she nodded.

"All the more reason to partner up with me," he said casually, bending to retrieve the balls he'd hit. "Everyone expects me to flunk out, so if you manage to succeed it'll be all the more cele-bratory."

"I don't think everyone expects that of you." She scurried to pick up the ball that had bounced off the green, and placed it in his hand. "I, um, I have something for you in my car."

Myles lifted a brow.

"I'll go get it." She began to step away.

"I don't need anything."

"It's a peace offering."

"I don't need one." A gift would pierce him, hook him like a trout. He'd struggle, but ultimately be unable to break the line.

She tipped her head, staring him down. "Maybe I need to give you one."

"We tee off in a few minutes."

"The clubhouse is always late in making the day's league teams."

He really didn't want a peace offering.

"Please? Just come to my car and we can put it in your truck. Then you won't have to carry it around."

"What is it? A bunch of balloons?"

"Please?"

He stared at her for a long moment, then with a dramatic sigh followed her, unsure what he was getting himself into, but pretty certain he was already hooked.

KAREN COULDN'T HELP FILLING the silence with nervous chatter as she and Myles walked to her car. The way his golf shirt tightened over his biceps was incredibly distracting. She unlocked her Honda and bent to collect the book from the backseat, then hugged the hardcover volume to her stomach, suddenly uncertain. What if this made things worse? What if he took it the wrong way?

But how could he not like the book? He'd said he'd enjoyed it even though it appeared he wasn't a big reader. However, she knew from experience it was often the act of finding the right one at the right time that opened up someone's entire world and made him or her a reader. Maybe all Myles and the other cowboys in town needed was the right book. If the community had more folks reading then maybe it wouldn't be such a fight to get adequate funding for the library each year.

"What do you have there?" Myles asked, his voice laced with curiosity.

Karen straightened, still clutching the book. "The illustrated version of *The Da Vinci Code*."

His blue eyes turned slate-colored, as if lightning was coming. Her mouth kicked into gear, her words running together. "You said you really enjoyed the references to the art, and I thought you might like this version because it has pictures of paintings and other things that tie in with the work, all right here in one convenient package." She thrust it at him with both hands.

Myles stared at her, the storm clouding his aquamarine eyes not receding quite as much as she'd like. There was no wind in the parking lot, and the heat radiating off the asphalt caused sweat to prickle her spine.

"You thought I'd like a picture book." His tone was flat, a warning.

"Yes! You said you'd enjoyed the story, and while this has illustrations, it's not a picture book. It's a book with... with pictures."

She'd offended him. It was as if her gift was reinforcing how she'd called him a dumb jock, when all she wanted to do was prove that she didn't think he was.

He'd fisted his hands at his sides, not taking the offering. "You think I *need* a picture book."

"No." Her heart was pounding hard and she flipped the volume open, turning so he could look at it over her shoulder. "What I like about this edition is that it has photos of the paintings referenced in the text. Like the *The Last Supper* by Leonardo da Vinci." She found the page it was on. "See? When there's that clue about Mary in the painting you can just flip here and see what the author is referring to." She turned her head to smile at him, and her excitement faded. Myles still looked insulted, his guard up.

"It's a lovely book," she said weakly, feebly holding it out again. "It made me think of you and how you made an effort to talk to me about it."

Myles finally reached for the offered book, and she forced herself to gently let go.

It was as though the entire world stopped breathing as Myles cracked the spine and the pages folded open, glossy and rich. The birds remained quiet. No cars entered the lot. No mowers purred in the distance.

"I don't think I've ever been given a book before."

Was he pulling her leg?

"Not since I was seven, maybe." He was solemn, turning the colored pages.

Cowboys really didn't care for books, did they? She saw so many come into the library, look around as if they'd accidentally entered a foreign realm, ask for the computer corner and never take out a book. Never express one iota of interest about anything other than the machine that would help them print off a grant application, file their taxes or search for something they couldn't figure out from home.

How could these stoic men, who spent so much time alone, not want to have their quiet worlds opened up like she had when she'd been an isolated kid? Her parents had been dedicated to her older sister's cheerleading career, so from an early age Karen had been carted around to events across the globe, stashed in the bleachers for hours while her sister practiced or competed. Books had literally saved her, since she didn't possess the coordination to be a cheerleader herself. And maybe a part of her had wanted to stand out, be opposite to her sister, who was all about her sport. Whatever it was, Karen could only imagine how alone she would have felt without books in her childhood.

Myles dragged a finger across the painting of *The Last Supper*. He gave it a thoughtful tap, then glanced up at her. "You know, I wondered about this part."

"You didn't look it up?"

He gave a slow shake of his head. "Didn't occur to me."

"Oh."

"Thank you."

She nodded. "I hope you enjoy it. Except you already read it, so you probably won't want to again." She turned to lock her car, berating herself for the awkward peace offering. It was like buying someone a full-course meal right after they'd finished one. Plus books didn't really seem to be on his radar. Karen often got chided for pushing them on people, and here she was, doing it again.

"I didn't read it."

She turned as his words registered.

"It was the first book that came to mind other than the football one," he said. "I knew you wouldn't want to talk sports, so I tried to find something we might have in common."

"You thought you could have a conversation with me—a librarian—about a book you hadn't actually read?"

"Nobody accuses me of brilliance." He gave a smile that bordered on devilish, and she realized he was flirting with her. His lying about the book had required more effort than most men made, even if it was misguided. "Ryan had been talking about the story at length, and I felt like I'd read it. He went deep into English-teacher-analysis mode. It was interesting."

"I thought he taught math and physics."

"He had an English class last spring." Myles was clutching the book with both hands as if it was something precious, and she hoped she'd found him the key that would open the world of reading to him. "Thank you for thinking of me."

"I'm truly sorry for what I said last night."

He gave a one-shoulder shrug. "Sometimes I take advantage of my reputation." He flashed her a smile that quickly died. "But if you do want help with the library, my offer is genuine."

"And so is my fear of failure." She pocketed her car's fob and began walking back to the clubhouse. There was no way she could pull off a fundraiser of that size. As president of the student council in the eighth grade she'd tried raising money for the school library by holding a used book sale in the lunchroom. The jocks had come through and upturned her table and called her a nerd. While she didn't think anyone would do that in Sweetheart Creek, she really couldn't see a community of cowboys getting behind a library fundraiser.

"What would be worse?" Myles asked, falling into step beside her. He smelled like the earth after a rain—fresh and alive, she noted. "Trying and failing, but knowing you tried and gave it your all? Or failing without trying, and knowing that maybe you could have pulled out a win?"

"Is that what you say to your players?"

"It's like Wayne Gretzky says."

"The hockey player?"

"You miss one hundred percent of the shots you never take."

"Are you telling me to take the shot even though I'm not qualified?"

"I'm not your coach. I don't know your skill set. But as a spectator in the stands, I'm cheering for you."

They'd stopped on the deck overlooking the fairways.

"Are you?"

"Pick your team. Find people who have the strengths you lack and make it happen. I believe in you, Kitty."

Her heart swelled with gratitude, but she wasn't sure if it was from the way he was backing her, or from the new nickname and how it made her feel special.

3

*M*yles hid his reaction when he was placed on the same mixed doubles team as Karen. He'd been put with Jackie Moorhouse and his brother Ryan, who had arrived at the last minute.

"I didn't know you were coming," Myles said to his brother as they collected the score card and their clubs.

"Yeah, thanks for asking if I wanted a ride."

"We could have all carpooled," Jackie said, joining them while flashing Karen a grin. Jackie was decked out in a golf skirt and short-sleeved top, and it strangely suited her.

"We're playing best ball?" Ryan asked, referring to how the players would each tee off like in regular golf, but the teammate whose ball landed in the better position would be declared the best ball. The other teammate would then take their ball over and hit from that position as well.

"Two against two," Myles confirmed.

"Karen and Myles—y'all are a team," Jackie said. "Ryan and I will try and defeat you."

"That shouldn't be too difficult," Karen muttered.

"Be prepared to get creamed," Ryan said.

"I was born ready," Karen muttered again, her expression one of defeat.

"Yeah, yeah, yeah," Myles grumbled, not in the mood for smack talk from his brother, either. Not only was Karen in his group, but she was on his team, meaning they'd be joined at the hip for the next nine holes. Yes, he had accepted her peace offering and was being a nice guy. But an hour and a half where they had to work together in an attempt to beat Jackie and Ryan, as well as the other teams out on the greens? That was too much to ask. He would be eating a fresh new chump sandwich by hole three.

"Go ahead and tee off," he said to Karen. "Ready golf. Whoever's ready first goes."

"I know what ready golf is," she said under her breath. She moved with halting steps toward the tee box, her expression one of sheer dread. She placed her tee in the short grass, then balanced a bright pink ball on top, her long fingers hesitating as she let go as though expecting the ball to roll off its perch.

She stepped back for a few warm-up swings, exhaling loudly as though trying to quell her nerves.

"I'm not very good," she warned, not looking at him.

"That's fine."

"For real."

"She hit a squirrel out of a tree last week," Jackie said.

"I did not!" Karen said hotly, finally looking up to glare at her friend. "It jumped to a new tree. That's all."

"And hit the ground."

"It jumped!"

Myles bit down on his cheeks to hide his smile.

Karen shook her head and focused on the ball again. She positioned her feet, relaxed her shoulders. She had good form, and Myles figured she likely wasn't as bad as she feared, but was nervous about making a good impression.

He took a moment to size up Ryan and Jackie, who were

goofing around—well, Jackie was and Ryan was trying to avoid her—instead of warming up off to the side. Karen said something about cowboys, then repositioned herself with what was obviously a well-practiced routine, like she was going through a mental checklist.

Everyone remained quiet during her backswing, and she let out a muttered curse when her ball sliced to the left, bounding toward a grove of trees. Myles tried to hide a smile below the brim of his ball cap as she stomped off the tee box. He'd finally found something that Miss Perfect didn't excel at. Other than catching footballs.

"Trying too hard to impress your teammate?" Jackie asked her, smirking as she passed Karen on her way to tee off. "Normally you hit much better than that."

Karen turned deep red and avoided looking his way while snapping at him, "Don't you dare laugh at me or I'll stick this club so far down your throat it'll come out your back end."

Ryan choked on a surprised laugh, but Myles squelched all feelings of mirth, sensing that Karen's verbal warning was brimming from an old need to protect herself. But from what? Did she really think he would laugh at her? Then again, he knew not everyone was kind when it came to an inability, and he felt himself soften toward her in empathy.

He glanced at Jackie for insider info, but she simply shrugged and waved him off after mouthing "*She hates golf.*"

"The next shot will be better," Myles assured her, wanting to reach out and give Karen's arm a reassuring squeeze. "You just took your eye off the ball."

"I'm sure that's exactly what happened." Jackie wiggled her shoulders, her club loose in her grip as she glanced over at the men. She gave Myles a wink.

He smiled back, but didn't egg her on like he usually might. His brothers took Jackie and her flirting too seriously, but Myles knew if he wanted to send her running all he had to do was accept one of her playful advances. Her entire game was predicated on him saying no or running away.

After Jackie and Ryan teed off, Myles took his shot, driving the ball two hundred yards, setting it down just shy of the green.

"Have you been coming out here to practice?" Ryan asked, grabbing the handcart that held his clubs. His shot had been decent, but hadn't gone as far. He was strong, just not quite as big as Myles, whose extra power helped him on the links. At least when he lined up his shots properly. When he didn't he could really drive his ball into trouble.

Myles slid his bag onto his back. "Nope."

"You disgust me," Ryan said, and Myles noted how Karen shifted uncomfortably.

"It's just a game," he said to her, hoping to put her at ease. He got the impression that she was not only a perfectionist, but also a bit competitive, and hated feeling as though she might be letting him down.

"You're a chip and a putt away from making par," his brother stated.

Myles shrugged at the suggestion that he might start their game off with a great score. "We'll see."

"Have you noticed Hernandez seems off?" Ryan asked, referring to their team's quarterback. Blake Hernandez was lined up for scholarships and it wouldn't be long before college scouts would be permitted to start having conversations about all those big-league promises they used to lure seniors to their schools.

Myles shrugged. "Just an off week?" A week that had gone on for several games, now that he thought about it.

"The season's too short, especially if he wants scouts calling him."

"And we want to make State." The goal was ever-present in the back of his mind, the conversations around town always circling to the annual Texas football championship match held in the Dallas Cowboys stadium, which, so far, the Torpedoes hadn't managed to win. "We can start increasing Rodriguez's field time." The sophomore who would replace Hernandez after he graduated had some serious potential.

"Good idea. That way if Hernandez chokes or starts making bad calls again we have someone ready to step in."

"I was thinking that new kid Finnegan might have some promise as a quarterback as well. He's smart and quick on his feet."

"Yeah?"

Myles shrugged. His brother, currently possessing more qualifications, was the head coach and made the bulk of the strategy calls while determining field time for each player. However, when Myles shared his thoughts Ryan tended to listen.

"Let's try him in some drills."

Decision made, they hurried to catch up with the women, who had their golf bags strapped into their rented handcarts and were moving quickly. Jackie was giggling, Karen groaning and complaining about some guy making it all look easy. Myles would've loved to overhear what they were discussing.

When they came close to where Karen's ball had bounced, he asked, "Want to play my ball?"

His was the obvious choice, as it had landed with a short, clear shot to the hole.

"Yes," she grumbled.

"Need help finding yours?"

"No."

Moments later she found it near the oaks and holly, and brought it to where Myles was waiting. They'd both hit from there, then from where whoever's ball landed closest to the hole.

Myles hit first and overshot the green, his ball disappearing over the side and no doubt bouncing into some difficult terrain. Karen hit next, but her swing was off. Her ball bounced forward a few feet and stayed put.

"That'll work," he said, moving up to it.

"Don't laugh at me."

"I'm not. That's actually better than my shot."

"It's a bad shot, Myles. Yours went farther."

"Farther, but into trouble. Let's play yours." He dropped a new ball beside hers, planning to retrieve his original ball later.

"Myles, don't." There was an edge to her voice he hadn't heard before.

"Don't what?"

"I read the book. I know how to play golf, and your shot was better."

"This is real life, Kitty. Not some book." The nickname seemed to frustrate her more rather than calm her like he'd hoped. "I've learned from experience on this course that more, shorter hits in a straight line are better than long shots that land you in tough spots."

"You don't need to placate me."

He leaned lightly on his club, and narrowed his eyes. "Why would I placate you over a little white ball?"

"Mine's pink."

"Why, Kitty?" The woman needed to retract her claws and trust him a little. Would that kill her?

"I know I suck, okay? I know you won't win today, and the guys will ride you about it, and it'll all be due to me being your partner." Her face reddened again and her jaw tightened.

"Karen, I don't care if I win. It's just a game."

"You don't need to try and make me feel better. I'm a big girl." She began hauling her cart toward his ball.

"How many shots do you think it'll take to get my ball out of the rough?" he called, digging in. She was so sure she knew who he was and how he was feeling right now, and she was dead wrong. Maybe it was *his* competitive side wanting to hit her ball instead of his, because it truly was lined up better. Or maybe it was just wanting to wipe from her brain that false perception of him as some unkind jock.

"Your ball," he called, "even though farther away, is well positioned and will take fewer shots to get onto the green."

Karen narrowed her eyes, glaring at him over her shoulder.

"Come here." He waved her back. "I'll bet you dinner you can get this ball into the hole from here in three shots or less."

She laughed.

"Okay, fine. I'll buy you a book."

That caught her attention.

"And if I win, I buy *you* a book?" she asked, changing direction.

"You already did."

"A person is allowed to have more than one, you know," she said, coming to stand next to him.

"Really? Huh. I'll have to remember that." A smile teased her lips as well as his, and he felt the tension between them slacken. He lined up his shot, hitting his ball up onto the green, then stepped aside, gesturing grandly. "You try."

Her shoulders dropped and she took the few steps to her ball. She had a nine iron, but what she really needed was a club with more angle so the ball would go up and plunk onto the green instead of overshooting into the rough, where his first ball had landed. He quickly grabbed a new club from her bag and handed it to her.

"Try this one." When she hesitated, he said, "Come on, I read it in a book."

"Did not." There was a hint of a smile again, but she took the club and made a few practice swings.

"Less force. More like this." He gently swung his club to demonstrate. He'd love to stand behind her, wrap his arms around her frame and help her with the timing of her swing, but he had a feeling she might not appreciate that.

She watched him for a long moment, then grudgingly began practicing her swing again.

"Keep your head down." She kept looking up too soon.

She grumbled and stomped up to her ball, then hit it up onto the green right near his.

"Great shot," he said, raising his hand to give her a high five.

She looked in surprise at her ball, then at his face. Tentatively she lifted her white-gloved hand, slapping his.

"It's only the first hole," Ryan said to Jackie as they joined them on the putting green. "We can still kick their butts."

"I don't care who wins. I'm here for the scenery." Jackie batted her eyelashes at Ryan, who quickly looked away. Myles chuckled and winked at Jackie, who flashed him a seductive grin.

Karen, who was lining up her putt, caught the smile and wink, then struck her ball at the wrong angle and sent it shooting off the green into the longer grass. "Sorry."

"Don't worry about it," Myles replied.

"So how did you cowboys end up playing golf?" Jackie asked. She was making a big show of adjusting her putting stance, which involved a lot of wiggling her backside.

"We wanted to get into the NHL," Myles said.

"The National Hockey League?" Karen asked in disbelief.

"I remember that!" Jackie stated. "You boys were hockey crazy for years."

"Yeah, but our parents got tired of driving us the hour and a bit to San Antonio to practice skating every week," Ryan said. "They told us that golf was pretty much the same thing, and that hockey players golfed."

"Seriously?" Karen asked, watching Myles with interest.

He nodded. "You gotta have a dream, right?"

"Didn't you get laughed at?"

He shrugged. Hockey wasn't what the kids had chosen to laugh at him about.

He angled Karen's cart handle toward her. They had completed the hole with a great score, beating Ryan and Jackie by one stroke.

"So do I owe you a book, or is it the other way around?"

Karen asked him with a shy, proud smile that looked good on her.

He shrugged. "Double or nothing on the next hole?"

"I don't even know what we're betting on."

He gave her a grin, taking her cart for her. "I don't either, but it's fun."

She stretched her back, hands on her hips, inhaling the warm fall air. "It is, isn't it? And such a nice day for a walk."

"Too bad for the pesky balls we're chasing, huh?"

She laughed, that rich one he loved so much, and he knew he'd relaxed her as well as earned her trust.

As they headed to the next hole, Karen asked, "So why the NHL? It doesn't even snow in Texas."

"Hockey players are cool!" Ryan exclaimed, from where he and Jackie were trailing behind them.

"Sexy," Jackie interjected, giving a little shoulder shimmy.

"A friend from Houston, Maverick Blades, got in."

"True." Myles had gone to visit Maverick during the summer and had been floored by his gorgeous beach house in Galveston —a stone's throw from where Maverick had grown up, but in a whole different pay grade when it came to the neighborhood.

"The five of us were going to play for Colorado so we could move there and learn to ski," Myles said, remembering how they had spent hours mapping out how they'd all make it into the NHL. The difficulty of getting time on the ice to play the game hadn't been a deterrent, and they'd figured playing street hockey in their spare time was close enough.

"You Wylders are an interesting lot," Karen said as they reached the next tee box. "How did you ever think you'd get there? I mean…" She opened her arms, indicating the beautiful rolling hills of the golf course. "No snow. No ice. No arena in town. Is it the jock mentality to assume everything you want will come easily to you—even the impossible?"

Myles snapped his head in her direction. He'd assumed he'd

see scorn and ridicule in her expression, but she seemed genuinely curious.

"We told everybody we knew, and they did whatever they could to help," Myles said.

"Christmas was the best." Ryan's face lit up at the memory.

"Everyone was heading into the city to shop," Myles explained. He often thought that, as the youngest, the hockey dream had likely been a highlight of Ryan's youth, since it was one of the rare times all five Wylder brothers had played together. "So whoever was heading that way would drop us off at the rink for a few hours. The hardware store even ordered equipment for us."

"But after telling everyone and accepting help, didn't you feel like you had to keep going with the dream?" Karen asked.

"Not really," Ryan said.

"Didn't they tell you how impossible it was?"

"We were kids," Myles replied.

"They probably knew our dreams would change," Ryan said.

"And they were likely just happy to support us doing something healthy that didn't lead to trouble," Myles added with a laugh.

"And," Jackie said, "we all wanted to know y'all 'way back when' in case you stubborn crazies actually made it into the NHL."

Karen, her expression calm and quiet, turned to Myles. "Is there anything you can't do? Anything you're afraid of?"

He felt a familiar shame dogging him as he processed her question, one answer coming to mind.

"Everyone has something."

PLAYING golf with Myles was distracting. It didn't help that Jackie kept pointing out how handsome he looked in his golf attire, and how strong and fit he was.

It also didn't help seeing him hang out with his brother. The two were obviously close, and the story about the boys wanting to join the NHL, then bonding to work toward that dream, even though they'd fearlessly failed, was inspiring and heartwarming.

Those crazy Wylders had told the entire town they wanted to do something absurd. A bunch of boys living far away from snow and ice didn't just want to participate in an ice sport, but to dominate it at the highest professional level. That was either stupid or gutsy. A week ago she would have voted for the former. Now she wasn't so sure.

Myles was surprising her, too. She'd expected him to laugh at her lack of skill and refuse to take anything more than her minimum required number of "best ball" shots as they team-played their way down the fairways. Instead he was relaxed, willing to offer suggestions—many of which had already improved her game—and made her feel as if she was a valued and capable part of their team. Plus they were winning.

He was causing her to warm to the sport.

But the NHL anecdote and how Sweetheart Creek had supported them? If she didn't know better, she'd say that story was the universe telling her to suck it up in regards to her cold feet about fundraising for the library. Then again, a town full of cowboys? Why would they help her fight to save the library? It was on the chopping block for a reason.

"Did he like the book?" Jackie whispered, as they walked to the third-to-last hole.

She nodded. "I think so." Myles had accepted her peace offering after his initial hesitation, and she felt as though he might truly read the book.

"He has pretty good golf etiquette for a cowboy," Jackie said, elbowing Karen and sending her and her pull-cart a few steps down the side of the hill they were angling up.

"Fine. I'll consider Myles." She was kidding, but she did wonder if flirting with him would get the attraction out of her system. There had to be a deal breaker in his personality. Something that would help her move past her infatuation as she got to know him better, so she could find her true Mr. Right. After all, Myles Wylder was a jock as well as a cowboy. Those types of men were into being rough and tough, while she was into things more refined. That alone should be a deal breaker.

She applied the handbrake to her cart at the seventh hole and pretended to look for a fresh tee. As she crouched beside her bag, she undid the top button of her shirt. Feeling obvious, she fingered the button, doubting herself. She should spend a bit more time thinking about the implications of flirting with Myles before she jumped in. Yes, he was hot. Yes, he made her feel like a superstar out here. But long-term? There was nothing between them that would last.

"Karen? Need a tee?" Myles asked.

She bolted upright, dropping her hand. "I'm ready. I'm good. Thanks. My turn?"

She approached the tee box and went through her routine, breathing deeply to calm herself. How was it that just thinking about flirting with Myles got her so wound up? She'd undone only one button on her shirt and felt as though she was flashing the man. Jackie had two buttons undone. *Two.*

A button wasn't a kiss. But she'd bet his kisses curled a woman's toes in the most delicious way.

"You okay over there?" Myles asked. She was staring at her ball, and jerked as awareness set in. How long had she been standing here, mooning, while the others waited for her to proceed?

"Just visualizing a straight shot," she said, after clearing her throat.

Jackie giggled and Karen's cheeks heated.

The seventh hole was a tricky one, with water and sand hazards, and quite a few trees bracketing the fairway. The golf course designer had definitely possessed an evil streak, as a badly aimed drive could cost them points. Despite her improvements, Myles had been carrying the team more than she'd like.

"Take your time," he said.

Karen swung her club back, then whacked the ball as hard as she could. At the last second, she lifted her head to see where it was going to go, ruining the shot. The ball sliced off her club and into the trees to the right. She groaned and allowed her shoulders to slump. More trees.

"I'm sorry," she said to Myles. "At least we took my required three drives earlier." Today's Best Ball rules stated that they had to play the ball from three tee-offs from each player on a team, even if it wasn't the best hit of the two.

"Don't worry about it," he answered easily.

No laughter, no mocking, just kindness. The man knew his way to her heart, didn't he?

Well, except he was going nowhere near her heart.

As he passed her on the way to the tee box, she caught a hint of his shampoo or soap as well as his calm and confident smile. What would those lips feel like against hers?

Jackie had focused on Ryan. "You should get socks like Myles. Look how they emphasize the definition in his calves. They're nice, aren't they, Karen?"

"That comes from working out, not the socks," Myles grumbled.

"I'm wearing the same socks," Ryan stated, his tone flat.

Karen giggled. "They look very nice on you, too," she assured him.

Myles hadn't called her Kitty again, and she was curious what it would take to have him do so.

"My apologies. It's all you. All pure, tanned and brawny,"

Jackie said to Myles, who was still lining up his shot. She said to Karen, "Have you seen him push those big bracket things across the football field?" She fanned herself, eyes twinkling with mischief, and Karen felt the heat, thinking about Myles out on the field with his team.

With rounded eyes, Myles turned to face them, obviously perturbed.

"He's not a piece of meat, ladies," Ryan said. "And I'm pretty sure you're both breaking the rules of golf etiquette right now. I could have you reported."

"No, we're fine," Jackie said, casually waving a hand. "Karen's undone only one of the buttons on her shirt. She has to undo at least two more before we get close."

Moments later there was the distinct sound of a golf ball cracking tree branches off to their right. Myles yanked his broken tee from the turf, his expression strained as he stalked off the tee box, his eyes going straight to the top of Karen's shirt where the button was undone. His eyes dipped to button two and three, and it was all Karen could do to not cover up the small triangle of skin she had exposed.

No wonder men didn't find her sexy. She couldn't show even a small bit of flesh miles above her cleavage without feeling as though she was out of her element.

"So? Going to the next barn dance?" Jackie asked cheerfully, walking down the fairway with Ryan. Both their shots had been beautiful, and Karen wondered if Jackie had intentionally messed with her head, then Myles's, to give her team an advantage.

Wordlessly, Myles and Karen took their clubs and headed toward the trees.

"Don't be party poopers! Smile!" Jackie called with a laugh.

"I know what you were doing, telling us that NHL story," Karen said when they were halfway to the tree line.

"What?" Myles asked. He was walking close to her, his steps matching hers.

"You were showing me it's okay to try something gutsy in Sweetheart Creek. That the community will step up and support me if I pursue something publicly, such as fundraising for the library. That it's okay to dream big, then fail."

He stopped, his eyes on that undone button. "We didn't fail, Kitty." His gaze lifted. "We just changed our focus. And I'm not suggesting you do anything foolish."

He'd called her Kitty again. Was this something he did only when they were alone? She liked that idea. She needed something cute to call him. What was a nickname for Myles?

Kilometers?

She sighed. She really needed help with acting flirty.

They'd reached the edge of the trees, and Myles said, "Ladies first."

Karen set the brakes on her cart and took several steps in, Myles behind her. She heard a rustle in the tall grass to her right. She froze, afraid it was a snake. Myles walked into her, automatically wrapping his arm around her to steady them, his hand splayed across her stomach. When he didn't release her, the heat from his midriff pressed into her back.

For a long, surprised moment they were silent and still. Then Karen turned slowly, her body tight to his. To her surprise Myles was looking at her like he was a doomed man as his face inched lower, coming closer to hers. She slid her hands to his shoulders, over his strong, taut torso, and shivered, knowing she might not get a chance like this with him ever again. Her fingers found their way into his hair, knocking his ball cap askew. His lips were close to hers and she could feel the heat from his breath as she went up on her tiptoes, her mouth meeting his.

WHAT WAS HE DOING? Hadn't Myles persuaded himself that anything to do with Karen Hartley was a bad idea? And if he had, why was he in the bushes, kissing her like they were a couple of teenagers?

Then again, none of his teenaged kisses had been this good, and none of the women had felt like Karen.

In the distance he could hear Ryan calling to ask if they needed help. Myles lifted a hand from Karen's petite waist, waving away his brother even though he was pretty sure Ryan couldn't see them through the trees.

Karen stirred in his arms as if she was going to break the kiss, and Myles pulled her tighter. She opened her mouth, deepening their contact and sending his world spinning. His hand bunched the material at the small of her back, tugging it from the waist-band of her shorts. He circled his palm in a caress, taking the fabric with him. On the next circle he could slide his hand against the warm flesh there.

"You two okay?" Ryan called, his voice closer, and Karen jolted in Myles's arms. He ignored his brother and continued kissing her, his hand finally reaching bare skin. She sighed into his mouth even as footsteps came through the bush, breaking branches. They suddenly halted, and after a long pause Ryan murmured, "You know? Maybe Jackie and I will finish up this hole without you." The steps retreated.

Karen finally broke away, inhaling deeply. She had been tugging at his hair, and Myles's nerve endings were firing.

He wanted more.

She went to step out of his embrace, and he tightened his grip again, angling his head to give her one more wet kiss.

Then, not wanting her to have to push him away twice, he forced himself to release her.

He *definitely* wanted more. A lot more.

He had felt the press of her chest against his, the warmth of her back, the way her tongue had swooped through his mouth, wet and firm.

His hat had fallen into the grass and he scooped it up, buying time so he didn't do something rash like angle them against a tree for support as they took their kisses deeper.

He had a feeling that, for her, the episode might have been merely a moment of weakness, even though he was already trying to sort out how to get a million more of them. He wanted to pull her back into his arms and see if the next kiss would be as good.

Something rustled beside them, and Karen just about jumped into his arms. "Snake!"

"You see it?" He nudged her behind him, wishing he was wearing his cowboy boots. The hard leather could stop a bite, but these ridiculous golf shoes and short socks weren't going to do much if a copperhead or rattlesnake decided to defend its territory.

"No." She hustled out of the bushes, high-stepping like a hurdler.

Myles paused where he was, listening. Hearing nothing, he slowly made his way out of the trees to where Karen stood, arms wrapped around herself, eyes on the grass near his feet.

"Shall we take a stroke for a lost ball?" he asked, grateful that his voice sounded normal, casual. All about the game.

"Yes," she said primly, smoothing her golf shirt, then swiftly tucking in the hem with a red face.

"Your shirt looks good with that button undone," he said, hiding his smile until he had his back turned, even though it would mean missing her reaction. He pulled a new ball from his golf bag and dropped it near where his earlier shot had gone into the woods.

Technically, depending on which rules were in play, he probably should've taken his ball back to the tee box. But right now he wanted to expedite things, so he could see what Karen did when it was time for them to say goodbye.

They caught up to Ryan and Jackie, who had already teed off

on the next hole. The two were unsuccessfully hiding their grins, and Ryan gave Myles a subtle nod of approval.

"You know, I think I probably need to go back sooner than the rest of y'all," Jackie said, as they were finishing the game. She turned to Ryan. "Is there any chance you're leaving early, and could give me a ride home?"

"Sure."

"Karen you can give Myles a ride back?"

"Ryan and I both drove," Myles said, chuckling at Jackie's attempted set-up and her fallen expression. Karen scowled at her friend in warning, her cheeks a delightful pink.

Myles shook hands with everyone as they headed back to the clubhouse, leaving Karen for last. He put an arm around her shoulders, squeezing her against him as he said, "Thanks for being my partner. It was the best round of golf I've had all season."

She gave him a prim look that tickled him no end. "Wasn't it your only game?"

"Maybe. Still the best, though."

"Your flattery…" She gave a mighty sigh.

He slowed their steps so she'd look at him. "Who says I'm using flattery and not simply speaking the truth?"

Her face went red again.

"Did y'all ever find those balls that went into the woods?" Ryan asked, his voice a higher pitch from trying to mask his mirth.

Karen's eyes grew round, and Myles laughed.

This woman was likely to kick him out of her life at any moment, but he was going to enjoy being in it while he could.

As they walked to the clubhouse, Karen hurried to catch up with Jackie. "We can leave early if you need to."

"No, it's okay. I'm fine."

"It's no problem. Really. If you need to be somewhere, we don't have to stay."

"It's okay, Karen," Myles said seriously. "It's not like Jackie's taken you to a football game. You're still safe with me." He winked at her and Ryan let out a guffaw.

"Well, I guess that's a good thing, then," Karen said. "Planning a wedding on top of a fundraising event would be too much for a perfectionist such as myself."

"You're going to save the library?" Jackie asked, her voice excited.

"That's a fantastic idea," Ryan said quickly. "I know a lot of people who would help you out." He turned to Myles. "Isn't our cousin Nick's girlfriend big into libraries and fundraisers and stuff like that?"

"Polly? Yeah, she's raised millions of dollars," he confirmed. Polly Morgan was currently living nearby on their cousin Alexa McTavish's ranch, Blueberry Creek II. "She's helping Alexa raise money for her horse sanctuary."

"Isn't that where the proceeds from last night's barn dance went?" Karen asked, and Jackie nodded.

In other words, Polly was likely pretty busy at the moment. Not that long ago, Nick Wylder had been living and working on the Sweet Meadows Ranch, until Myles's dad had told him it was time to find somewhere new. The ousting had been a long time coming according to Brant, but it had visibly upset Levi. Although, in retrospect, leaving the ranch seemed to have been the best thing for Nick. He'd found a serious girlfriend, and Alexa was ecstatic about having a verified ranch hand working for her.

"Are you going to do the fundraiser?" Myles asked Karen.

She put her hands on her hips, studying him. "You never give up, do you?"

"Not when it's for a good cause." Or when it was for a woman he couldn't seem to get out of his mind.

4

*O*n Monday morning Karen ran her clammy palms over the thighs of her tan pants. She pulled her chair closer to the long, slightly wobbly table in the back room that the library board used for their monthly meetings. She gathered her file folder and neatly restacked the papers inside before closing it. She clicked her pen, then clicked it again before setting it down.

Only a month ago she had sat in this same chair, the one with the hole in the arm's upholstery, and kept her chin up while being told by the board that her job, as well as the entire library, was on the line.

But today she hoped to propose a way to save the facility. Something about hanging out with Myles yesterday had made her feel as though she needed to take the chance. She was nervous, though, worried that she wasn't prepared enough for any upcoming questions. But mostly she feared that her half-baked plan was laughable. That *she* was laughable for daring to think she might be able to do it. She wasn't even the head librarian, just a part-time staff member.

"Hello, Karen," Maria Wylder said, taking a chair near the end of the table. She was part of the volunteer squad for the library, and often attended meetings to offer the perspective of a patron and community member. Her support was always invaluable, as she knew how to get things done and win people over without ruffling feathers, and Karen wished she'd had time before the meeting to fill her in on her plan.

"Hi, Maria."

"I hear you were golfing with Myles yesterday. He said you're quite good."

"What?" She stared at the older woman, waiting for the punchline.

"He said you're new to the sport, but have a great analytical mind for it."

"I do?" She couldn't quite figure it out. Myles, a verified athlete, was talking about her sporting ability with his mother with no apparent irony or humor?

"Are you enjoying it?"

"Yesterday was fun," she admitted. She hadn't left the links nearly in tears, which had happened on other occasions when her frustration over her low skill level had clashed with her pride and competitive side out on the course. It might be the first time in weeks that Jackie wouldn't have to badger her into returning next Sunday by reminding her how much money she'd sunk into the sport already—and would lose if she gave up now.

People filed into the room, taking up the available seats, and Karen's nervousness increased as Henry Wylder, their interim president, took a spot at the head of the table. Laura Oakes's aunt, Luanne Blackburn, had been their president for years and had always kept meetings lively. Karen couldn't help but think the woman had somehow been shielding the library, keeping its doors open, as it felt like a coincidence to have it threatened so soon after her passing.

Henry called the meeting to order and quickly began running through business so they could be done by the time the doors opened to the public at eleven. Why he served on the board was a mystery to Karen. He was grumpy, and seemed to hate the library and everything to do with it, as well as resented the money it took from the town and county coffers.

"Karen, you asked to add something to the agenda?" Henry's cheeks puffed as he addressed her, his flyaway salt-and-pepper hair waving in the building's air-conditioning.

"Yes." She sat up straight, perched on the edge of her chair. "As we all know the library is facing financial issues and is likely to close within the year unless funds are found. I would like to make a proposal for a fundraiser."

Maria appeared interested, as did MayBeth Albright and Jenny Oliver. Henry narrowed his eyes and gave a small shake of his head.

"It's unlikely you'll be able to raise enough money in such a short period of time," he said gruffly.

Maria made a show of checking her watch. "I say we have time to hear ideas. Even keeping the doors open for an extra month is one more month our patrons can take advantage of our services."

Henry grudgingly gave a flick of his hand, permitting Karen to proceed.

She cleared her throat and glanced at Maria, who gave a small smile of encouragement.

"The idea of a fundraising gala was presented to me by a community member."

"Galas are expensive. There isn't time to put one together, and a black-tie affair is not Sweetheart Creek's style. You should know that by now," Henry said.

Karen felt her mouth drop open.

"Oh, come now, Henry," Maria said mildly, addressing her former uncle-in-law. "Women love a chance to get dressed up."

"And love spending all of a man's money in one night," Henry said with a harrumph.

"Right now the library is in such a state we can afford to entertain every idea brought to us," Maria said kindly.

Henry folded his arms and sat back in his chair, his familiar scowl set in place.

"Henry presents a good point," Karen said smoothly. "A gala might be a little too formal for a small town. But really, anything that gathers the community together can work. There are also garage sales, books sales and other things we could do."

"A garage sale? Do you have any idea how much money we need?" Henry asked.

"As a volunteer," Maria said, raising her voice, "I'm willing to help the library if a fundraising proposal was accepted. We have an active group of volunteers who would be happy to help."

"Thank you," Karen said gratefully. "Other community members have also spoken up to say they'd like to help." She cast a shy glance at Maria, wondering if she knew Myles was the big push behind her fundraising idea.

"Like who?" Henry demanded.

"Myles Wylder—"

The old man let out a bark of laughter. "He couldn't find the library to save his life!"

"Hey now, that's my son you're talking about," Maria chided.

"Does he even have a library card? He doesn't even read!"

"A volunteer is a volunteer," Maria retorted.

Karen swallowed her desire to drift out of the room. "Jackie Moorhouse and Ryan Wylder have also volunteered."

"Are they a thing?" Jenny Oliver asked, leaning forward, her green eyes sparkling with interest.

"I know Jackie's been chasing him for years," MayBeth said, sliding her reading glasses further up her nose. "Good for her on snagging him."

"I don't think they're more than friends," Karen said quickly, concerned she might be starting rumors.

"So y'all have a few volunteers for an undecided fundraiser?" Henry smacked his lips drily. "My, you've been a busy bee."

"People are concerned about losing the library," Karen said. "They want to help."

"Why they do beats me," he muttered "The building is old and nobody reads any longer. It's time to move into this century."

Karen bit her tongue while mentally counting the months until the next board election, until a voice at the other end of the table said, "I put forth a motion that fundraising options to save the library be gathered by Karen Hartley, and that she be free to spend up to two thousand dollars as seed money."

"Two thousand!" Henry practically exploded, slapping the tabletop as he lurched forward.

"Too much?" the woman asked innocently. It was Jenny. She leaned onto the table to see Karen. "How much do you think you'd need to get the ball rolling?"

"We're not having a ball!" Henry cried.

"Tell me about it," Maria muttered.

Karen did some quick math. She was tempted to suggest a few hundred dollars so Henry would look like a scrooge if he said no. But if she didn't ask for more, she wouldn't be able to put together something significant enough to meet a worthy target.

"Two thousand might be a bit more than we'd need at this time. We definitely don't want to put in more than we know we'll get back." Diplomatically, she turned to Henry. "How much would the board be comfortable putting forth?"

"Don't you go losing money we don't have," he declared.

"Yes, sir."

"We could offer five hundred dollars," MayBeth, the treasurer announced. Catching Henry's incredulous expression, she added, "However, we can add a stipulation that every expenditure must be preapproved by the board, but that it can be done via email in order to expedite things."

"Shall I make an amended motion?" Maria said, when nobody spoke for a moment or two.

Karen held her breath. If the motion passed she would be given the green light to try and save the library, even if the very idea of being responsible for the future of her own job as well as several others filled her with fear.

MYLES WAS SORTING through equipment in the football storage room in the basement of the school, looking for a better helmet for their quarterback Blake Hernandez. The seventeen-year-old had been acting funny lately, as well as complaining about the fit of his lid. Myles figured he could solve at least one of the issues, and leave the rest for Ryan, who was better at the touchy-feely aspects of being a coach.

Whatever was bugging Hernandez, it was more than just a rough week on the field. His marks were slipping, too, and it was time to bring in a tutor, which was why Myles had texted Karen earlier.

Yesterday's round of golf had been fun, not just because of the stolen kisses in the woods, but also because their team had won a gift certificate to the country club's restaurant. Jackie was already arranging a double date for Thursday night. Ryan and Karen had protested that they didn't need to share the gift certificate, and that Jackie and Myles should go. That wasn't what he had in mind, and he was certain it wasn't what Jackie wanted, either.

"Knock, knock," said a soft female voice, and Myles turned to see who was in the doorway, even though he would recognize it anywhere.

"What's up, Kitty?" He loved the way Karen's cheeks turned a nice rosy color at the nickname. She obviously hadn't had a man make her feel special enough that she took the small things for granted. "Get my text about Hernandez needing a tutor?"

"We've already scheduled our first session."

"Thanks."

Karen hesitated in the doorway. "I talked to the library board this morning about your fundraiser idea."

"I hope you didn't tell them I'm behind it," he joked, worried that attaching his name might encourage them to be less supportive.

"They say I'm welcome to try and raise some money."

"How about a lot of money?" He ran a hand over the curve of the helmet he was holding.

"I started creating a plan." She came forward, opening a plastic folder. Inside was a printed list.

"I've got to dig through these helmets. Why don't you read me the highlights while I work?" He pulled a few more helmets from the bin, checking the sizes. They really needed a proper shelf to store these on. Maybe he could make a request. It wouldn't cost much if he built it himself.

Karen dusted off a small desk and perched on top of it, ankles crossed. She looked adorable and serious, her glasses perched high on her nose. It was all Myles could do to not press himself against the desk, slide her closer to him and kiss those glasses right off her face.

"What?" she asked. She had a pen balanced between her fingers and flicked it back and forth a few times, like a cat twitching its tail in annoyance. "You have work to accomplish. Get to it, mister."

"Slave driver," he muttered, shifting more helmets in the bin.

"I was thinking a used book sale could bring in up to a thousand dollars. A garage sale could bring in at least that much, depending on the donations. I have five hundred dollars to make posters, rent the community center and whatever else we need."

Myles smoothed the dust off a helmet and turned to her. "That won't bring in the money you need. And anyway, the church just had their annual rummage sale. Everyone's out of crap to give away. You need to think bigger."

The end of Karen's pen disappeared between her lips, and he turned back to sorting helmets so he wouldn't think about those lips too much.

Those kisses in the woods had definitely earned a spot on the week's highlight reel.

"These don't cost anything to run," she protested. "I can't put up money we might not earn back."

"You need to create an *event*. Something people will want to get behind."

"We just need to raise enough to keep the doors open."

"For how long?"

"What do you mean?"

"How long do you want the doors open for? A week?"

"Myles…"

He allowed his frustration to sound in his tone. "You need way more than a thousand or two. Beyond keeping the doors open, don't you need new books? More staff? Fix up the front of the building? That hole in the roof? Don't you want new computers or shelves? Maybe even a raise?"

His mom had mentioned the dire state of the library and it sounded like they needed about fifty times more than a garage sale could bring in. Karen needed to get past whatever was making her think so small and save the place.

"This year I just want to keep the doors open."

"Where's the danger in dreaming big?" He set the helmet on the desk beside her, then leaned in. "What's your number?"

Her face turned red and she sputtered, "That's none of your business." She slid off the desk. "Just because we kissed doesn't mean we need to get so personal."

"I was talking about your dream budget, sugar toes. Not the number of partners you've had." He hooked a hand on her hip, angling her to face him. "But if you want to get personal, I'm okay with that."

He dipped his head as if about to kiss her, and her eyes fluttered shut as he inhaled the scent of her neck. "You smell nice."

He stepped back, releasing her.

She was frozen to the spot, head tipped back, eyes still closed, hands up and ready to grip his shirt. Her eyes opened with a sharp blink when she realized she'd been set up.

Unable to resist giving her what she'd been anticipating, Myles bracketed her right cheek with his palm and delivered a long, deep kiss that clearly left her unsteady on her feet.

"Myles..." She breathed his name as he ended it. "We can't—"

He placed a finger against her lips. "There's no harm in liking this. So quit thinking and kiss me again, Kitty."

KAREN HATED HERSELF FOR DREAMING.

Myles Wylder had a string of ex-girlfriends who either looked like ex-cheerleaders or were. And carried themselves with the confidence and fierceness of a gorgeous rodeo pageant queen, because they often were that, too.

And yet she kept letting him kiss her.

She was not a cheerleader.

Nor a rodeo or any kind of pageant queen or princess.

But he believed in her. He'd set her up with managing the cheer team, which she'd ended up loving despite her initial hesitation at getting involved in the sport her sister had dominated for so many years during Karen's childhood. He also didn't hesitate to set her up as a tutor for his most important players, and he believed she could save the library. He didn't laugh at her attempts at golf, and had managed to win them a small prize— the first thing she'd ever won. Ever. He'd even lifted her in a big hug when they'd gone up to collect their gift certificate, making her feel as though she was special, as though anything was possible in her life if Myles was there nudging her along.

Which made him a little dangerous, especially when those facts were considered in combination with his divine kisses. He had sexy, stealth timing, making her wait for a kiss she wasn't sure was going to happen, so when he did kiss her it was all the more thrilling.

She pushed against his chest now, not wanting to end the kiss, but needing to. They were in the high school, and she couldn't get caught making out with the football coach. She could get fired for that.

Maybe. Probably not.

But it would be extremely embarrassing.

Especially since she and Myles would never become a couple, and she didn't need the mortifying wake-up call that she'd degraded herself into being yet another jock's conquest, like she had in high school because she'd allowed her need for attention to override common sense. Jocks did not go for book nerds, and she'd be wise to remember that she was nothing but a challenge for a man like Myles, who was used to women falling at his feet—something she steadfastly refused to do.

She gave him one more quick kiss, then pushed him away for real. "We can't."

"We just proved we can," he said with a smile, not letting her go.

"I have a job."

"So do I."

"I'd like for us both to keep them."

That seemed to sober him up. He stepped away and she immediately missed the warmth of his chest pressed against hers.

She cleared her throat. "So? Dream bigger? What did you have in mind?" And why was she thinking of everything but fundraisers right now?

"I don't know. A gala."

"They said no."

"Or a festival."

"A festival? In November?"

"A fair. Whatever. You know. Games like a dunk tank, cotton candy. Corn dogs."

"Do you know how much work and expense that would be?"

As though sensing her reluctance, Myles said, "Do you know how long it will take for another librarian job to come up within commuting distance if the library closes?"

The truth was like a slap, and Karen hugged herself, thinking. He was right, of course. But there were so many risks with putting together a big fundraiser. There was no money to front any reasonable-sized event, and if they didn't at least break even she'd look like a fool.

"How do we do this then?" Desperation was clawing at her, and it wasn't the kind that made her want to pounce on Myles when he took his time landing a kiss upon her lips. She shoved her hands through her hair before remembering she had it up in a bun. She let out a huff and paced the room. It smelled like old equipment and teenage boys.

She looked up. "Can we go somewhere else to brainstorm?"

"Afraid I'll kiss you again if we stay?"

Yes.

"It smells."

Myles inhaled, brow creasing. "True." He flashed a quick, toothy smile. "Smells like victory?"

She rolled her eyes and he laughed.

"Let's go." She walked to the door, Myles following, the red helmet dangling casually from his fingers. He owned this room like he owned the field. If the library was her place in the world, everything to do with football was his. "What position did you play in high school?"

He locked the storage room door, saying, "Linebacker."

"You must have been good." He had the breadth for it, the

patience. Let the opponents think you were coming for them, then drop back and wait them out, to make them think they could make it through to the end zone. Then when they let their guard down, thinking they might make it past you, you took them out. Her father had taught her that during some of the rare moments they'd spent together—naturally, in front of the TV watching sports.

"You were in cheer?" Myles asked.

She shook her head.

"But Rhonda said you know a lot about it?"

"My sister was a cheerleader."

"And you weren't because…?"

"Because she was." And because Karen didn't have the flexibility, coordination or interest. Maybe if her sister hadn't been so into it, she would have tried it for fun. But knowing she'd always be a very distant second in that arena, she'd chosen something different for herself—books.

Myles made a thoughtful humming sound, watching her with those crazy blue eyes of his that looked like the Mediterranean Sea.

"Let's go brainstorm in the diner," she suggested, before he could delve into her psyche.

"You're hungry?"

"They have big tables so we can spread out our ideas." The Longhorn Diner was also rife with gossipers. That would help prevent her from getting drunk on his steady gaze, which held lust and attraction and all those other dangerous things.

"Or we could talk and drive. Do you ride horses?"

"I thought you wanted to save the library?"

"I do my best thinking when my hands are busy."

Was that her imagination, or had his gaze just slipped across her body as if his hands wanted to follow that same trail? She shivered and clutched the neckline of her shirt, unsure whether she felt exposed or just plain sexy.

"Let's go to the diner," she said, trying for a cooler tone that would hopefully create a bit of distance between them. "You can take up knitting with the club of old gals in the back corner if you need to keep your hands occupied."

MYLES HAD CONVINCED Karen to come out to the ranch instead of going to the diner. She wanted to brainstorm, and he'd be more help to her if he was moving around while thinking and talking.

Plus he figured not being in the diner increased his odds of getting another kiss.

They had taken separate vehicles, parking in front of the ranch house, then walking around to the machine shed out behind the two stables to see what sort of random scraps they could use for raising money. Or at least that was his plan. Karen was still firing tons of small ideas at him. They weren't bad, but weren't going to get her close to the dream-big-and-save-the-library number he'd encouraged her to spit out.

"Guest authors?" she suggested now. "People pay to hear their readings? Or signed books donated by publishers and authors that we could put in a silent auction?" It was as though a valve had popped on her ideas spring. But she was still thinking too small, too safe.

"I'm listening. Keep going," Myles said, sorting through a pile of plywood leaning against a wall behind his mom's no-longer running Mustang. The wood was left over from past projects and repairs around the ranch, and they might be able to make something of it, but what? A stage? A kissing booth to set up on Main Street during the town's monthly auction day? He'd spend a lot in the name of the library if Karen was inside the booth.

It took him a moment to realize she had gone silent. She was resting on the running board of an old tractor, looking dejected. Bucket, Myles's black lab and Rottweiler mix, meandered over to console her, resting her large head in Karen's lap. Her fatigue seemed to lessen as she stroked the dog's ears and nape.

"What's your name?" she asked.

"That's Bucket. Usually she goes by Buckey."

"Buckey," she said softly. "I like that."

"Brant found her with a bucket stuck on her head."

"You poor thing." The dog sat for a moment longer, panting and absorbing all the love she could, before wandering off to see what she could chase in the yard.

"I don't know," Karen said eventually. "If we had five grand to put into a big event it would be easier." She inhaled slowly and Myles did, as well. The shed smelled like dirt floor, old oil and memories. Did she smell the same things as he did?

"Car wash?" she suggested.

"Get out your white shirt and pink bikini."

"My bikini isn't pink," she stated, giving him a direct look that made him imagine what color her bikini might possibly be, and whether he'd get a chance to see her wearing it.

"I build birdhouses," he said.

"That's nice," she answered listlessly.

"The bigger ones sell for quite a lot. I use scrap lumber from a builder near Riverbend. The only thing I have to buy are screws, and I have plenty. I could donate the proceeds."

"Don't you usually donate them to the football team?"

"Usually," he admitted. For the past few years he'd used the funds for team-building activities in early September. The guys would do something like go-carting for a few hours on his tab, then join the cheerleaders for pizza back at the school.

Karen shook her head. "The kids look forward to it."

"The concession at the football games has been doing really well this year. I'm pretty sure the teams would do okay without my couple hundred bucks. The kids could also chip in."

"I can't take that money."

"Dunk tank."

65

Her gaze turned toward him in confusion.

"There used to be a dunk tank in town when I was a kid." An idea was coming to Myles, building in his mind. "They used to bring it out at fairs." Why didn't Sweetheart Creek hold fairs any longer? They had been so much fun, as well as popular.

His brother Levi's shadow filled the doorway as he walked past, and Myles called, "Hey, Levi! Do you know what happened to that dunk tank that was around when we were kids?"

His brother leaned in the doorway, a streak of grease across his right cheek. "Ask Mrs. Fisher. By the way, I think the wind-mill's fixed finally. We can move that herd back whenever." He noticed Karen, and gave her a nod. "Hi, Karen. I hear the four of you are going on a double date Thursday night."

"That Jackie," Karen said in exasperation, shaking her head. "Myles won a gift certificate to the country club restaurant at golf yesterday."

"*We* won a gift certificate," he corrected.

"Jackie finally settled on Ryan, did she?" Levi asked with a hint of a smile.

"It's not a date," Karen insisted. "For any of us. Could you really see Myles going for all of this?" She gave a laugh, gesturing to her pretty, buttoned up blouse, which was still remarkably clean despite their location.

"Why not?" Myles asked, and her eyes widened behind her glasses.

"You're a jock." Her tone had become prim, her spine straightening. "And a cowboy."

"And...?"

"I don't think I'm your type." She wouldn't meet Myles's steady gaze, and he was afraid what she might think his type was. She looked at Levi, chin raised. "It's not a date. Trust me."

"Okay," he said, his tone hinting at disbelief.

"What is it with this town?" Karen asked, once Levi was gone. "Seriously."

Was it really that unthinkable that the two of them might get together? Myles wondered. And what was wrong with an athletic cowboy, anyway?

He pulled out his cell phone and punched in the number for The Longhorn Diner. "They just want everyone to be happy."

"Married, you mean."

"That, too."

Mrs. Fisher picked up the diner's phone and said in a stern voice, "I told you if you don't like the lawn the way I do it, then fall off your wallet and hire someone. The government gives you a disability check for a reason."

"It's me, Mrs. Fisher. Myles Wylder," Myles said, feeling as though he'd just walked into the middle of a domestic dispute. "I'll send Brant over to do your lawn."

"Sweetie," she said, her tone instantly softening, "there's no need. Really. William's just being a grumpy old man because he can't do the things he once could. Don't you go worrying about a thing. The way I do the lawn is fine. He just needs to let off some steam."

"You're on those pretty little feet of yours all day, Mrs. F., and Brant has a lawn tractor. He'll come by and take a couple of swipes, and then if William's upset it's on us, not you. We don't have to live with the man."

"Myles Cameron Wylder, it's an official Sweetheart Creek mystery as to why you're still single."

"Did I tell you you're looking lovely today?" he asked, pouring on the charm as Buckey bounded into the building, before tearing out again to chase Levi's dog, Lupe.

The older woman laughed. "You can't even see me!" She lowered her voice as though parting with a secret. "But don't you let Karen Hartley hear you talking to me that way."

Myles's gaze instantly darted her way. She was making marks on her list, her brow furrowed in concentration, the silver ring on her finger flashing as her hand flicked over the page.

"And why is that?" he asked Mrs. Fisher.

"No reason," she said innocently. "Just that if a gal has her sights set on a certain someone she might get upset if his sweet words were directed at someone else."

"You'll always be my number one, Mrs. F."

She laughed again. "Neither of us ladies are your type, sweetie."

He found himself sighing involuntarily. How many times was he going to hear that today?

"Now did y'all call me up for something? Or did you just have a sense that I needed some sweetening up after the day I've had?"

"Anytime you need someone to brighten your day, gorgeous, I'm your man. But I did call for a reason, actually. I was wondering if you knew where that dunk tank went to. The one they used to bring out at the town fair. Is it still around?"

"Oh, those were the days, weren't they? Lemme see..." She paused for a second. "I think Clint might have it at his garage." There was a muffled sound as she covered the phone receiver. He could hear her ask, "Maria, hon, does Clint still have the dunk tank?"

"My mom's there?" Myles asked. And why would she know whether Clint had the tank or not?

"She says she saw it sitting at Clint's."

Levi had gotten upset a few weeks ago at the idea that Clint Walker and their mom might be sweet on each other, but Myles hadn't really seen that happening. Now he wasn't so sure.

"Did she see it at his home or at his garage?" he asked carefully.

"Clint has it, dear. Now, what do y'all need it for?"

"Thanks, Mrs. F. I'll let you know if we have a plan for it, so you can help spread the word."

He ended the call, and said to Karen, "It looks like you're going to need to get out your not-pink bikini—and your white shirt—because I found the dunk tank."

"No." She shook her head calmly. "It looks like you're going to need to get out *your* white shirt, Myles. Women would pay a lot to see through that wet fabric." She gave him a sly smile that would pretty much guarantee he'd agree to anything. Including volunteering to fall into a dunk tank full of freezing water.

"Well then," he said, lowering his voice as he leaned closer, "be prepared to raise a lot of money for the library, Kitty, because things are about to get wet."

5

On Wednesday after school Karen watched Myles's large hands strap her into a harness for a bungee trampoline they were considering borrowing from his ex-girlfriend Daisy-Mae Ray, for their impromptu library fundraiser.

Things had snowballed after Myles found the dunk tank, and ideas had come fast and furiously, with a fair planned for the weekend after next. He'd already secured the tank, plus some beanbag and ring toss games, and borrowed a popcorn machine from the bank and the cotton candy machine from the school. Betty Coulter, the Sweet Meadows Ranch riding stable manager, had agreed to bring in some horses for children to ride. The new owner of the ranch next door would bring some goats for a small petting zoo, the cheerleading team would do a few routines, and there would be a book sale as well as a small farmers market.

So far their costs were minimal, with Myles calling in favors every time Karen turned around. The problem was this zero-gravity thing he was strapping her into. She'd vetoed the idea even before she'd heard it belonged to Daisy-Mae, and that she would lend it to them as a personal favor rather than charging like she normally would.

Right now the woman was standing in her scrubby front yard a quarter mile off the highway, her hands on her hips, her skirt barely long enough to cover her butt. She had the plumpest breasts Karen had ever seen in real life, and would be best described as sex on a stick. Except there was no stick. Just pure gorgeous, sexy woman to make Karen's stomach roll with envy, just like it had when Daisy-Mae had danced with Myles last Saturday.

When they'd arrived, though, Myles had barely looked Daisy-Mae over before shucking her clinging hands and asking to check out the ride.

Even though Karen protested that the trampoline was a lawsuit waiting to happen, Myles had chosen her to be the guinea pig. Probably because, unlike Daisy-Mae, she was wearing pants.

He'd wrapped his large, strong hands around her waist and lifted her onto the platform, then commanded her to step into the harness. Too stunned to run back to the safety of his truck, she'd begun listing all the reasons she shouldn't try the ride. Until he'd kissed her long and hard, bunching her shirt at her lower back like he couldn't get enough of her. Still dazed from the kiss, she'd let him position her where he wanted.

The man didn't fight fair.

"You can't make me jump once I'm all strapped in, you know," she informed the top of his head as he adjusted the buckles. Apparently she was smaller than Sex on a Stick. Maybe because she was so short. Myles and Daisy-Mae were almost the same height and would make babies so hot they'd combust the entire world. The idea of the two of them getting back together seemed to be something Daisy-Mae wouldn't mind, judging how she'd been on Myles at the dance like cheese on ham left out in the hot Texas sun.

Watching them, Karen had felt the two were a good match, but the more she was around Myles, the more she realized there was more to him than she'd first assumed. Yeah, he was hot and kissed in a way that made her feel like it was a sin, but there was something else, too. Something she couldn't quite figure out that made her think Daisy-Mae might not be what a man like him truly needed.

Done adjusting Karen's thigh straps, Myles tightened the belt that went around her waist, his hand brushing her right breast in the process. He continued on as though not noticing, but she saw his jaw flex, his eyes dart to hers.

"Sorry," he murmured.

Feeling she needed to speak so she'd stop thinking about how awkward yet nice the accidental brush had been, she pulled on the bungee straps angled from her waist to the scaffolding above. "How easy is it to transport this?"

"I've taken it down a time or two."

A seductive retort was on the tip of her tongue, but she bit it back, afraid she'd unleash the beast she'd spent the past few days trying to coax back into its pen. One waving checkered flag would have Myles racing right back into their dangerous flirting. She didn't need to kid herself that their suggestive banter meant more to him than it did. He was Mr. Easy Come, Easy Go. Whereas she was Miss Long-term, always looking at where a kiss might take her.

Or maybe it wasn't her pulling back that had caused him to ease up on flirting today. Maybe it was because that flame had already burned out, just like it had with Sex on a Stick, who was now sitting in the shade looking bored. Maybe Karen wasn't that attractive to Myles. After all, what man kissed her like he had, but then apologized while accidentally brushing her breast?

A gentleman? Or a man who'd moved on?

She closed her eyes, trying to end the cycle of berating herself she had slipped into. He was a nice guy who was helping her. There was no need to analyze everything. Why couldn't it just be working together and sometimes kissing?

She felt warm hands grip her shoulders. "You okay?"

She opened her eyes to find Myles had bent his knees to bring himself face-to-face with her. His eyes were that amazing mountain-lake color again. Did they change with his mood? She kind of felt like they did.

"I'm fine. Just going over my routine. The one I'm not going to perform because dying isn't on my bucket list, and I'm as coordinated as a box of screws. I don't know what you think you're going to accomplish having me strapped into this thing unless you feel, for some sadistic reason, that I need to be tortured."

Myles gave her a crooked smile and adjusted his cowboy hat, inadvertently reminding her that he was not what she was looking for. No cowboys. No jocks. A golfer, maybe. But not him.

She sighed. She didn't even know anymore. Maybe she'd be better off giving up and becoming one of those boring-old-librarian stereotypes who talked about her cats as if they were her children.

As Myles gripped Karen's harness, giving it a tug to ensure it was secure, she hated to think what the cost of Daisy-Mae's favor to him might be. Or how personal.

"Sure you want to do this?" Myles asked.

"Who wouldn't want to die in this contraption today? It's so gorgeous out." She looked up at the tower above and the bungee lines that attached her to it. She gave them a tentative tug, worried she might pull one of the metal support beams down on her head. "Should I be wearing a helmet?"

"No."

"This is safe, right?"

"Yes."

She stared at Myles for a long moment, unsure what the next step was now that he'd gotten her strapped into this thing. Pretend she was going to barf so he'd release her? Jump around and try to look coordinated?

"Why are we testing this out again?"

His eyes connected with hers as he stepped forward, and she thought he was going to kiss her again. She tipped her face up in anticipation, unable to stop herself. His hands, which had lifted slowly to cup her face, gently took her glasses, tenderly pulling them off.

She was in rough shape. How did having her glasses removed feel like such a sensuous move?

"Sure you're okay?"

She nodded, frowning sternly. "Of course. I manage cheerleaders who do stuff like this every day. It's easy. Just do what they do."

It wasn't easy, though.

Not for her.

Myles folded her glasses, leaving her ridiculously disappointed for a reason she couldn't quite isolate among all the swirling feelings running through her.

Sex on a Stick called, "Just relax and have fun."

"I'm not going to jump," she said, loudly enough for Myles to hear. She gave Daisy-Mae a little wave and a smile. She felt dressed to the chin in her track pants and cheer team athletic tee, compared to Daisy-Mae, who wore her cleavage like a badge of honor, a small tattoo of a yellow rose over her left breast.

Why didn't she have a tattoo? Or wear a low-cut shirt? Wouldn't it be nice to have someone like Myles trail his gaze hungrily over her form?

The problem was she would end up with men she didn't want doing more than that. She had learned that the hard way as a teenager, when she'd been in the process of discovering her sexuality. Apparently it hadn't just been for her to discover, but for others, too. Namely, a few jocks who thought, quite rightly, that she would love the attention.

She'd quickly learned that the attention and affection weren't real, and that it was a lot better to lock it down until she found a man she could trust and was actually interested in. Then she could show a little here and there without finding herself in a situation that would make her the class laughing stock.

Karen was standing in the middle of the trampoline, lost in thought, Myles still in front of her. He grasped the bungees like he was going to give them a big downward pull.

"What are you doing?" Karen asked in panic.

"Getting you started."

"No!"

He yanked down hard, his knees bending, his arm muscles rippling, his shoulders flexing in a mesmerizing way. Then suddenly he let go, sending her shooting into the air. She screamed.

"Keep holding the cords," he called.

That shouldn't be an issue. She was fairly certain her finger joints had permanently locked around the rubber bands that were lifting her up, up, up into the beautiful blue sky. Sex on a Stick called something about a backflip. As Karen descended smoothly, her feet touching the trampoline, the give and take of the rubber and mesh netting sent her into orbit once more like it was the most natural thing in the world.

"Just tip your weight back. It's easy!"

They were already going to mock her for the screams that kept being ripped from her, and she mentally shrugged, tipping her weight back. Another bloodcurdling scream ravaged her vocal cords as she performed what felt like a perfect backflip.

Karen squeaked in surprise. Really? Her? She wasn't a gymnast. Her sister was! She'd seen it performed a million times, and now she'd done it. With assistance of this contraption, of course, but it had been *so* easy.

She did another one. Then on her next bounce flipped herself forward.

Now she understood why her sister had enjoyed gymnastics, tumbling and cheerleading. It must feel this fun and easy for her. This was why the cheerleaders didn't want to come off the field until their legs were too tired to hold them up. Karen jumped again, tucking her knees in for a forward roll, keeping her grip on the bungees like Daisy-Mae was instructing from her spot in the shade. The cheerleaders were going to love this ride!

She continued spinning and jumping until Myles called to her, "You gonna come off that thing sometime before you lose your lunch?"

"Nope!" And anyway, lunch had been eons ago. She was fine.

"Okay," he said agreeably, and began chatting with Daisy-Mae in the shade.

"We should have a pie eating contest," Karen called out to him. "And mud wrestling!"

Myles laughed. "You going into the mud?"

"I'm serious. Write those down." She continued to do forward rolls, followed by back rolls. She was getting tired, but the exhilaration of being able to do cool stunts pushed her to keep going. "Pig races." She did another high jump, marveling at how her legs could shoot her so far. "It won't raise a lot of money, but it'll be fun."

"How about a kissing booth?" Daisy-Mae called.

"Only if Myles is in the booth," she replied.

Daisy-Mae laughed. "I'd pay for that."

"I'm not doing it," Myles said, his voice hard. "There's only one woman I want kissing these lips, not the whole town."

Karen felt a warm ball grow in the pit of her stomach, but it wasn't from the flips. It was because she knew Myles was referring to her. Not Sex on a Stick, but Plain Jane Karen, aka Kitty. *His* Kitty.

IT HAD TAKEN Myles almost ten minutes to convince Karen to get off the zero-gravity trampoline. Then another five to convince her that he really didn't want to sit in a kissing booth at the fair.

Did she?

No, she did not. Thank goodness, because while he didn't want anyone kissing him if it wasn't Karen, he sure didn't want anyone else in town kissing *her*.

A kissing booth was out of the question, but mud wrestling and pie eating contests were not. Karen was in the groove now, the trampoline seeming to have loosened things inside her, and she was throwing out ideas on how to make the event even bigger and better.

Her grin was as wide as the cab of his truck, her eyes sparkling as they headed back toward the school, where Karen had left her car.

She massaged her thighs with the heels of her hands. "My legs are like Jell-O from all that jumping."

"Had fun?" Myles asked.

"I want one for my backyard."

"Careful," he warned, "the top button of your shirt might come undone if you keep having so much fun."

"You think you're so funny," Karen said, blushing, her hand automatically going to the neckline of her rosy-pink athletic T-shirt. He'd stolen her away from cheer practice, and she looked sporty, and pretty hot.

"You were great up there."

She turned her gaze to the window, watching the dry pastures go by.

"What sports do you play other than golf?" he asked.

"I don't." She turned to him. "Why did you tell your mom I'm a decent golfer?"

"You are."

"Why did you tell her that, though?"

"You think I'm playing a game?" he said, after watching her expression for a moment.

She shifted uncomfortably.

"Why do you think you suck at sports?"

"I do."

"I have yet to see that."

Her cheeks reddened again as she stared at him. He winced, remembering the incident in September.

"Sorry about hitting you with the football. I thought you wanted to play."

"Why would I want to play?" Her tone was hard, yet curious.

"You looked left out." She blinked at him as though he'd seen something she hadn't expected, and he continued. "You had this look like you wanted to play. You know, join in, be a part of things."

"I did feel that, but I didn't want to be tossed into the scrimmage." She shook her head, giving a quick, exasperated sigh. "And that wasn't an excuse for you to throw a ball at me as hard as you could."

He started to deny it, but she added, "I was only curious what it would feel like to be confident in… just— Never mind. You wouldn't understand." Her hands fluttered in the air, her moves agitated.

"I think I would."

She gave him a frown that said *Yeah, right*.

"I didn't mean to hurt you."

"You're not the first person to humiliate me with a ball." She had crossed her arms and was looking out the window again.

"Well, I'm sorry I did. I'm passionate about sports and I want to share what I feel with others. Sometimes I forget."

"Is that why you shoved me on the trampoline today? You forgot?" She was staring at him through those big glasses of hers. When he'd pulled them off earlier it had felt sexy, like he was removing something intimate from her body. The trust she'd shown letting him do that had nearly undone him.

"Did you?" she insisted.

"I guess so."

They rode in silence for a mile. When he turned north toward town, taking them off the gravel road onto pavement, he asked, "Did you get laughed at in school?" It was a hunch based on how she expected him to react to her sometimes, and he confirmed it in the way her eyes darkened. "It was by a jock, wasn't it?"

Her lashes fluttered as she inhaled, again confirming his hunch. It hurt that she was lumping him into that group—jocks who would laugh at and mock their less athletic classmates, but he knew the type. They were ruthless and relentless, and he'd found himself the brunt of their jokes on a few occasions. But he'd thought his actions would have proved to Karen by now that he was different.

"You know…" He squeezed the steering wheel, not sure how to tell her he understood her pain without revealing why he wasn't as fond of books as she was.

"Do I know what?" she asked, when he left his words hanging there.

"Oh, no you don't," she scolded when he remained silent.

"Don't what?"

"Jocks and cowboys can express their feelings without losing a piece of their manhood." Her tone was soft, prodding, humorously cajoling.

"I wasn't going to…" He waved a hand as though confused by her accusation.

"Yes, you were." She gave him a smug smile he was pretty certain was intended to goad him.

"You're using stereotypes as a shield," he accused in frustration. "I thought book lovers were supposed to be open-minded and accepting." He took a corner into town too quickly, rocking her toward the door.

"Then prove me wrong."

Now he had to share his feelings or he'd be fitting into that stereotype he was trying to convince her didn't fit him? Oh, she was good.

"Fine. You want to know something? Jocks laugh at everyone, Karen. Nobody is special or saved, or sheltered from experiencing that. Nobody."

"You got laughed at by jocks?" She chuckled, then caught his expression. "But you're good at sports. People like me get mocked and nailed by the ball."

The idea of Karen getting intentionally struck by a ball explained why she'd been so upset when he'd accidentally hit her back in September.

He turned to her briefly, mouth open, but no words came out.

"People like me are picked for teams last," she said. "Not people like you."

"I wasn't picked last, but I still got laughed at."

"For what?" She was curious; he could see it in the way her crossed arms had relaxed, how she was leaning his way.

"I wasn't good at school."

"But isn't it a badge of honor if you fail to reach the top of the class? Aren't sports the be-all and end-all in the world of jocks?" Her voice took on a harshness that coated what he knew to be long-buried but not forgotten hurt. "I mean, they flip over tables of books when the student council president tries to run a book sale at lunchtime to raise money for the school library. They're definitely not into thinking nerds are cool."

She had tipped her chin upward, as though taunting him to deny her experience, her feelings.

"I'm sorry that happened to you, Karen."

She looked out the window again and murmured, "Maybe it didn't."

He knew it had. Her chin was quivering, and before she'd

turned away he'd seen fresh pain in her large eyes, as if all this had happened only a few days ago.

Myles tightened his fingers around the steering wheel as though it might help him keep a grip on his own emotions, his need to share that he knew *exactly* how she felt.

"You think I didn't get laughed at for getting answers wrong? Or for looking at a page in my textbook and not..."

He shoved the truck into Park in the school lot, his chest aching as he thought about the humiliation that had happened in the very building in front of him. His lungs tightened as he recalled how he'd look at the page, unable to make sense of the jumble of letters swimming there, while the class waited for him to read a passage out loud. The mocking and imitation in elementary school. Then in high school, the awkward silence that soon became nervous titters, then scoffing. Then after class by being jostled into lockers, and later, being called stupid on the field during practice.

Even being one of the best school athletes hadn't saved him from the humiliation. He'd learned to brush it off, act like reading didn't matter where he was going with the ranch and with football.

When Myles turned off his truck and glanced over at Karen, her eyes were huge with sympathy, as though she'd slipped into his mind while he'd been bashing his way down memory lane. He gave his head a firm shake and got out, unsure where he was going, but certain he wasn't about to sit in that truck—his truck —and be felt sorry for by a woman who thought he was the same kind of person who had made him feel the way he did every time he looked at that low brick building across the parking lot.

Karen slowly got out on her side, watching him. "Do you want to talk about it?"

He went to glare at her, but saw a glint of humor dancing mischievously in her eyes, and his anger faded. She was egging him on. That was ballsy.

He watched her for a long moment, studying her just like she was studying him. "You're a real pain in the butt, and yet I can't seem to stop thinking about you even though you're everything I've never wanted in a woman. You know that?"

She laughed, her eyes bright as she moved back toward his truck as though she planned for him to take her somewhere.

"I know exactly what you mean, Myles Wylder—exactly what you mean."

6

*M*yles watched Karen stand beside his truck as though waiting for an invitation. They'd only agreed to go to Daisy-Mae's, and since they'd done that, he'd returned her to her car.

But if there was one thing he recognized, it was when a woman didn't want to go home. He'd bet his truck that Karen wanted to continue to explore this unexpected feeling of being linked together by a mutual past of painful experiences that had molded who they were today. Somehow, despite being opposites in so many ways, they shared something he didn't share with anyone else, and that sense of connection was swamping Myles with a feeling of need.

A need to learn more about this mysterious woman he thought he knew. A need to take her on that double date with Ryan and Jackie tomorrow night. And also a need to set her up in his own private kissing booth and spend all his money on her.

"What's next on the fair-planning agenda?" Karen asked, placing a hand on the hood of his truck.

"Today?"

"Yes. What can we get crossed off the list, so we're further ahead tomorrow?"

Myles let out a long breath and pushed a hand through his hair. There were a lot of things to accomplish. They'd handed some tasks off to library volunteers, but there was a lot still on their own lists, since they didn't fully know what all they wanted yet. As for his agenda, it included everything from repairing the old games he'd dug out of storage around town, to plotting out some new ideas for activities. He found he didn't want to do any of them if they didn't include Karen.

"I have my to-do list, and I know you have yours." She moved to her car and pulled a sweatshirt from the backseat. "Even though I haven't seen yours yet."

Myles leaned against the truck's front fender and tapped his temple to illustrate where his list was stored.

She stepped closer, a bag slung over her shoulder and a playful grimace toying at her lips. "Lovely. That makes it so easy for me to reference while figuring out how much time we need for each task."

"Retract your claws, Kitty."

"I was joking!" She was standing near his truck again, shifting from foot to foot. "So? You said we needed to sort out some games?"

"I need to make some repairs on the beanbag and ring toss setups. They're a bit wobbly from being manhandled in storage, and I don't think they'd make it through a full day. I've already filled the dunk tank out on the ranch, and it only needs a willing victim to test it."

"Oh, darn." She snapped her fingers. "I forgot to pack my bikini this morning."

Myles's focus drifted toward her chest, his imagination creating unstoppable images. "How's your white T-shirt? That would do in a pinch, I'm sure."

"I didn't wear it. Didn't want to get it wet," she said, in a regretful, tongue-in-cheek tone.

"Guess you'll have to see me in mine then." He gave her a wink that caused her bottom lip to curve under her top teeth as she fought a smile.

"Lucky me." Her voice was throaty and she looked at him from under her lashes in a way that made his brain combust.

"Okay, let's go," he growled, getting into his truck before he did something spontaneous like pull her into a tight hold and kiss her senseless.

A few minutes later, as they turned down the driveway to Sweet Meadows Ranch, Buckey came running. She barked happily and settled into a trot beside the truck.

When they got out of the vehicle Buckey snuffled Myles's pant leg to check out where he'd been, before running around to Karen, who bent and cooed over her.

"I should let you know I'm not that great with power tools," she said, "but I'll do my best to be helpful."

"Are you bluffing like you did with golf?"

"I didn't bluff about golf."

"We won, didn't we?"

"Thanks to you!" She came around to his side of the truck and gave him a playful swat.

"Do you always sell yourself short?" He caught her hand, marveling at its petiteness. There was something about her size that made him feel protective.

"Myles, flattery will get you nowhere."

"Neither will lying to yourself." He reached into the truck, grabbing the backpack he'd wedged between the bench seat and the cab's back wall.

"I'm not lying to myself."

"Right. You suck at sports. I forgot, what with the flips on the trampoline and kicking everyone's butt at golf."

JEAN ORAM

"Anyone can do a flip on that machine and golf was due to you."

He gave her a look of disbelief while pulling out a coil-bound textbook from his backpack.

"Have you forgotten the bloody nose?" Her eyes seemed dewy and big behind her glasses, and he'd never noticed the smattering of freckles across her nose before.

"I *am* truly sorry about that."

"At least you didn't laugh," she muttered, wrapping her arms around herself.

"If power tools aren't your thing, you can read this to me while I work." He passed her the football textbook.

Karen frowned and turned it over in her hands, studying it. She looked up at him with her eyes narrowed. "Why?"

"Because I'm in the middle of taking a course, and putting together a community fair takes a lot of time. I can't do both things at once, so if you read to me while I fix the games, we'll be set." He gently guided her out of the way so he could close his truck door. She stayed where he'd pushed her, smoothing a hand over the book's cover with a look he couldn't decipher.

"Is that all?" she asked quietly. For a moment he thought she might be on to him with having her read the textbook to him, but when she looked up her expression was fresh and bright. "Shall we?"

And so, with the dog running ahead, they went to the machine shed, where Myles had unloaded the borrowed carnival games earlier that morning.

Karen perched on the running board of the tractor once again, rested the open book on her knees and began flipping through the pages. Buckey tried to find a place for her head in her lap, and without paying much attention, she lifted the book, alternately turning pages and petting her ears. "Which part am I reading?"

"Start on chapter four." Myles was about three chapters

behind where he needed to be in the course, although that wasn't the fundraiser's fault. He'd been able to keep up until early September, but then had slowly slipped behind when Levi had begun to ask more of him around the ranch. Levi had hired an extra hand recently, but someone had to train him, which was often left to Hank, their main hand, and to Myles. Soon they'd all have a bit more breathing room, but Myles worried he'd be too far behind in his course by then to be able to take the final exam in early December.

Karen began reading while he gathered his tools, her voice melodious. He had to concentrate to focus on her words, rather than the fact that she was reading about his favorite sport, her crossed legs in track pants, her glasses adjusted high on her nose. There was really nothing sexier than her in this moment as far as he was concerned, and he wondered what else he could convince her to read to him. If she was the one narrating, he was pretty sure he could focus on anything from astrophysics to the intricacies of romance novels.

She paused when he whacked at a broken support board, knocking it off the ring toss game so he could replace it.

Once he was done making a racket, she announced, "Pop quiz!"

He looked up. "I don't know your favorite color. I don't know your birthday. And I don't know if you prefer wine and chocolates or movie tickets for Valentine's Day. But I'm guessing pink of various shades, although maybe lavender." Her golf visor had looked smart on her, contrasting with her dark hair. "And I'd guess you were a spring baby, and that you'd prefer wine and movies. Preferably a movie that will make you think and cry."

She laughed. "*Football.* Have you been paying any attention at all?"

"So was I close?"

"Scarily so." She focused on the textbook, toying with its edges.

Myles leaned against the tool bench, brushing the dust from his hands. "Quiz me."

She straightened her shoulders. "If the coach suspects hazing is happening on his team should he—"

"Talk to the team players immediately as well as investigate thoroughly. Contact parents and involve school authorities if necessary."

Karen looked impressed, but didn't say anything, simply flipped a few more pages before asking a more technical question. He answered correctly and she shut the book, causing Buckey to go on the alert with a light woof. That drew Lupe to the doorway to give out a similar woof, which set off Buckey.

"Quiz is over?" Myles asked, after hushing the dogs.

"Teach me how to use the drill."

"I thought you were helping me with the class."

"You already know all of this." She set down the textbook. "Why are you taking this course, anyway? You obviously don't need it."

"I know it because you just read it to me." He walked to where she was sitting. Having her read was helpful. She'd already gotten through half a chapter in record time, and everything she'd read to him was sticking. "And I'm taking the course because it'll add another level to my coaching certification."

"And why do you want to do that? Ego?"

"No, it'll boost me up the coaching pay grid, which will allow me to help out here on the ranch by drawing a smaller income. Levi's stressed about money because the ranch supports us five brothers at various levels, as well as the retired generations. Levi's serious about Laura and soon they'll want to have kids. More mouths to feed."

He could see Karen was tracking what he was saying, and she was quiet for a moment. "Is this some sort of weird fetish then?" She narrowed her eyes at him. "Having me read football to you?"

"Do you want it to be?"

She turned bright red and the tip of her tongue lifted to rest against her top teeth. He wasn't sure if she was interested or apprehensive.

He edged slightly closer, inhaling the scent of her shampoo. "I thought you were helping, but if you want to turn this into something kinky, I'm game." He gave her a devilish smile, knowing it would flip her inside out with discomfort.

"Myles!" She shifted, her eyes a dangerous black.

He tapped her elbow, dropping his smoldering act. "Karen, seriously. Nothing weird is going on. I learn well by listening. Always have."

She watched him warily, not convinced. "Is that all?"

"Quiz me from the next chapter and you'll see I don't know it yet."

"You could fake it."

"I could, but I promise I will never fake anything with you."

She frowned, making a small huffing sound before finally saying, "Fine."

She repositioned herself on the tractor and opened to the last page she'd been reading. "But I'd better not find out you were messing with me."

She closed the book again, her thumb placed between the pages so she wouldn't lose her spot. "Does this mean you're able to remember everything people say?"

"Only the good stuff." He gave her a wink that sent her nose back into the book.

***

WHEN KAREN FINISHED READING the chapter, she looked up to find Myles had repaired both the stand for the beanbag toss as well as the one for the ring toss. He seemed to have sucked up every word she'd read aloud, while concentrating on restoring the two old-fashioned games. He might not be the professor type she normally sought out, but he had more going on upstairs than she'd first assumed.

And that could pose a hiccup in her plan of trying to kiss him out of her system. Obviously, it was proving to be a faulty one, because the more she got to know him, the more there was to be attracted to. And discovering that he was bettering himself with this class sure didn't help. Especially since he was doing it for his family.

Her stomach rumbled and she checked her watch, noting it was well past suppertime. "Are you hungry?"

Buckey barked and Karen laughed.

"She knows that word," Karen said.

"He does. And I am a bit." Myles sanded some edges on the game and stood back to look at his work. "Think we need to repaint this?"

"Do we have time?"

"Probably not." He had removed his cowboy hat and somehow looked more youthful.

"I'm helping at cheer practice again tomorrow," she said, drifting closer to him. "But I could swing by and paint it after."

"And I have football practice." He angled his body, giving her space she could slip into as she continued to drift closer. She loved how he didn't mind the physicality of her attraction, her need to be close to him.

She wanted to kiss him, but felt a burst of shyness, as though he wasn't hers to reach for. His left hand went to her waist, resting lightly, casually inviting her to come into his personal space. That wall she'd worked to build earlier in the week no longer felt like something she wanted to continue putting her energy into. His eyes danced over her face, the intensity of his gaze making her feel attractive, wanted. She placed her right hand on his chest and snugged her body against his.

"Thanks for helping me multitask," he said, his lips close to hers. He was so tall she would have to bend her head back even if he hadn't been wearing cowboy boots. He lowered his mouth to hers, lightly dusting her lips with a kiss that made her tingle with its gentleness.

"You're welcome."

He pulled her closer, deepening the second kiss. They were locked in an embrace when someone cleared his throat from the doorway.

Karen jumped back, smoothing her shirt. Myles had a way of gripping the garment at her back that made her feel as though he was wrestling with control, and she was certain she looked disheveled and thoroughly kissed.

Brant stood in the entry, looking amused yet sheepish. "I thought you might want to know that Polly Morgan was talking to Mom."

Myles grumbled, "I actually don't care."

"She's Nick's girlfriend," Brant said for Karen's benefit. She nodded, having heard her name mentioned a time or two. "She heard you're trying to save the library. She's an aficionado at raising money."

Karen's interest piqued.

Buckey, who had wandered out of the building, wandered back in and threw herself at Brant's feet, belly up. He crouched, giving the dog a good rub.

"Does Polly want to help?" Myles asked pointedly. Karen crossed her fingers. The more help the better.

"She figures a dinner and dance would go over well in Sweetheart Creek."

"That's a lot of work," Karen mused, picking up Myles's textbook. "And there are barn dances every other weekend already. Would anyone care to come to something like this, too?"

"Sure," Brant said. "Women like to be taken out on real dates. You know, where they don't have to bring the food."

"Run it the night of the fair?" Myles asked Brant, and he nodded as he rose from where he'd been petting the dog.

Karen's mind shifted into problem-solving mode. There was a long list of things they'd need to accomplish to pull off a dance.

"What's that?" Brant asked, angling his chin at the book in Karen's hands while edging closer.

"Myles is taking a course," she said absently, holding it up. They'd need to rent a place to hold the dinner as well as the dance, then deal with a caterer, tickets, volunteers, tables and maybe even dishes.

"You are?" Brant seemed surprised as he turned to his brother.

"Yeah."

"That's cool." Brant was watching Myles in a way that brought Karen's attention to the men. Taking a course was out of character for Myles, judging from Brant's expression, which was something Karen had concluded already. But obviously the class material was no issue for him despite his apparent dislike of reading. "Online?"

"Yup."

Brant glanced at Karen, then back to Myles, asking casually, "How's it going?"

"Guys," Karen said, feeling the pressure of the dance idea still lingering undecided in the air. "It's a course, okay? We have bigger problems. For a dinner and dance we would need to hire the community center, a band, find more volunteers, get a liquor license, find food, do up tables and decorate, make up tickets, advertise—"

"You know what the good news is?" Brant said, interrupting her.

"What?" Karen and Myles asked at the same time. He had pulled her close again.

Brant grinned at the two of them. "Polly just finished a bunch of fundraising for Alexa's rescue horse thing, and is bored."

"What does that mean?" Karen asked, her breath caught in her throat. Something big like this could possibly get them close to raising enough money—if they could find the cash to make the necessary deposits for the community center, band and caterer, of course.

"What?" she repeated.

Brant looked amused, and Myles gently tightened the arm he had around her waist as though afraid she was going to launch herself at his brother.

"It means you had better buy yourself a dress, Karen. Because there will be a very nice dinner and dance happening the night of your fair."

"It's in less than two weeks," she said.

"She knows."

"We can't. There's no way." How could she count on someone she didn't know to pull off something this important? If it flopped, the mud would be on her face, not Polly's. And she didn't have the time to make sure an event that big went off without a hitch. She was already strapped with preparations for the fair. Yes, the library board was happy enough for her to try and raise money, but it was practically on her own dime and her own time. Time that was also being eaten up by cheer, tutoring and her other librarian job.

Myles gripped her chin between his thumb and index finger. "Breathe, Kitty."

"I am breathing!" She needed space to think. She needed a calendar and a notepad. No, a time machine. Something like this needed to have been planned months ago.

"Kitty, listen."

She struggled to focus on Myles, who was holding her tightly.

"Polly pulled off a wedding for our dad in less than a week, while saddled with my cousin Nick as her helper." He paused to allow that to sink in. "She can do this. We just have to stay out of the way and hand her things as she needs them."

"This could really backfire."

"You can trust her."

Behind him Brant added, "She used to organize entire galas back in Canada. They raised a ton of money."

"This is for a small town."

"It's okay."

Looking into Myles's eyes, Karen felt her stress ebb. He was the action man. If he felt they could do this, then they could.

She let out a slow breath. And anyway, it was like he'd said. If it all failed she'd be moving out of town anyway, so there'd be no need to face the embarrassment for very long.

She inhaled, held it, then sighed and said, "Looks like I'm going to need to find a dress."

AFTER KAREN HAD STUMBLED across an old toilet seat in the machine shed and come up with a subsequent game where players had to toss rolls of toilet paper through the seat to win, Myles convinced her to go to the diner for a bite to eat. The place was hopping despite the late hour, which meant he had to play the good boy and not sneak in kisses despite his desire to do so.

After eating, as he gently pried Karen's fingers off the bill so he could pay it, he asked, "Are you really going to buy a dress for the dance?"

She leaned forward, her lips in a serious frown. "Will this actually work?"

"A dress? You have the legs for it, yes."

"Myles," she said, her exasperation showing. "Can Polly actually pull off something like a dinner and dance? There's a ton to consider."

"Dinner and a dance?" asked Mrs. Fisher, gliding past with a tray of pie. "I used to love going to those. Y'all fixin' to add one to the fair?"

Myles nodded.

"Oh!" exclaimed Jenny Oliver, the owner of the clothing shop next door to the diner, as she walked by their table, her straw-yellow ponytail swinging merrily. "Are you doing a silent auction or do you need some door prizes? I've got some fabulous new boots in Blue Tumbleweed I could offer, if you'd like. I've also been totally nerding out on all of these craft ideas online if you need help with centerpieces."

"That would be great," Myles said, giving her a grin. She winked and continued to the back counter to pick up her own supper order.

"Hey, Davis!" Mrs. Fisher called across the diner to a man wearing a T-shirt sporting the local radio station logo. "Put it on the news. There's gonna be a dinner and dance the day of the fair. We have less than two weeks to get the word out."

"Are the Torpedoes gonna win State this year?" Davis called back, lifting his focus from his steak sandwich special.

"Of course we are," Myles said, loudly enough for the man to hear.

"Then it'll be on the radio from dawn to dusk, and then some."

"We haven't got a band or rented the hall yet!" Karen said, her eyes round.

Mrs. Fisher turned in the other direction to call to a man with white hair sitting at the back counter. "Garfield? Are you still in charge of the community center bookings?"

He nodded, swiveling in his seat to face her. "What do you need, darling?"

"Pencil in a dinner and dance for the day of the fair, and do my husband a favor and stop calling me darling."

He nodded again. "For you, my dear, anything."

She rolled her eyes, a tiny hint of a smile tugging at her lips as she said to Myles and Karen, "You're set, kids. Except for food and the band. What kind of music do y'all want? Country and western, I hope."

"I think so," Myles said, noting that Karen still looked like a deer caught in the headlights of an approaching big rig.

"Hank's dating a gal," Mrs. Fisher said, referring to the Sweet Meadows Ranch's hired hand. "I think her dad is in that new band. They're really popular over in Riverbend."

"Really?" Myles asked. Apparently he needed to chat with Hank more while they were out doing chores each morning. Then again, they'd both been pretty busy bringing their new hired hand, Owen Lancaster, up to speed. But Myles hadn't even heard about this band from his grandfather, Carmichael, who, despite his retirement, still had his ear to the ground when it came to all ranch-related gossip.

"Ask for a word-of-mouth discount." Mrs. Fisher winked and moved to the rear counter to get Jenny's order for her.

"Thanks, Mrs. F. You're the best."

She called back to him, "Preach it, hon."

"You know I will."

"And ask your mother about that caterer she knows from the book club. She's got a good reputation and might float you the deposit if money's short."

"Thanks."

Myles gave Karen's hand a squeeze. She still looked a bit freaked out. "We've got this," he assured her.

She exhaled deeply and gave a slow nod. Knowing she'd fret until her mind was put at ease, like she had with the zero-gravity trampoline, Myles pulled his phone from his pants' pocket and found the contact he needed.

"Hey, Nick!" he said, when his cousin picked up. "How's it going? Any chance that smart girlfriend of yours is around?"

While Nick put Polly on the line, Myles handed his phone to Karen. "Talk to her."

Karen gave him a miffed look.

"What?" he asked.

"I'd like a little notice next time so I don't sound like a complete, unprepared idiot, thanks."

Mrs. Fisher was moving past and she lifted her eyebrows at

Myles. "Always the man of action, aren't you, hon?" She patted him on the shoulder. "Sometimes it pays to think first."

He laughed as she continued on. Like she was one to talk. She'd practically just planned their dinner and dance.

Karen introduced herself to Polly, and soon they were nattering on as though they'd known each other for eons. Seriously? Why the fuss? The two knew what needed to be done and spoke the same language of to-do lists.

Grinning, Karen got off the phone about ten minutes later, her eyes sparkling. So beautiful. She handed Myles his phone and he allowed his hand to rest over hers for a moment.

"This is totally going to happen," she said. "We're going to knock some socks off."

"Great."

"Polly's completely on board and knows exactly what to do. She said the caterer will take care of lots of the work, and that if you get a good one they practically sell the tickets themselves."

"You feel better?"

"I do." Her gaze narrowed, her smile almost predatory as she watched someone enter the diner. Myles glanced over his shoulder to see who it was.

Henry Wylder. His grandfather's youngest brother and the town grump. Myles looked back at Karen, who had tipped her chin upward, smile still in place as Henry walked past their table.

The man scowled, his gray-and-white hair an unruly mess as usual. "What do y'all have to smile about?" he snapped at Karen.

"Nothing," she said, her smile not dimming.

The man glowered, then turned to Myles. "You propose to her?"

"Nope."

"You know she's almost out of a job with the library. She's looking for someone to prop her up. That's all. It ain't love. You're just the first man with a steady pulse to come along and express an inkling of interest—even if you're a bit thickheaded for her tastes."

Myles held in a chuckle. "Thanks for the love life advice, Henry."

"It's not advice, it's the truth. Learn to use a dictionary, boy," he said sternly before stalking off.

"Isn't he a bag of laughs?" Myles said quietly.

"He was adopted into the family, wasn't he?" Karen said seriously, and Myles burst out laughing. His great-uncle had put a lot of people in town on the run with his moods, and Myles was glad the man had failed to do that with Karen.

"So you and Polly spoke the same language?" he asked.

The sparkle returned to Karen's eyes. "She's awesome."

"Should I call Hank and see about his girlfriend's dad's band?"

"Yes. And my dress is going to be so sexy your eyes are going to pop out." Her smile was sly in a way that stirred his blood.

"Promises, promises," he murmured.

She was leaning forward, hands flat on the table, excited by her conversation with Polly and the long list of things to organize.

"Actually," she said, "I think that was a threat."

"How can a sexy dress be a threat?" And what was her version of sexy? Wasn't a small-town event like this somewhat casual? Sort of like a barn dance, only with alcohol and no kids and no barn?

"You won't be able to think straight."

"I already can't."

"I haven't seen any evidence. You took my toilet paper idea and built it into a veritable game in less than forty-five minutes. That takes some straight-thinking skills."

"Trust me. As soon as you flash those flirty eyes of yours, Kitty, I can't think straight at all."

She laughed, her cheeks a pretty pink.

He stood. "We should go buy you a dress right now."

"None of the stores are open."

"Then we should watch a movie. Sit at the back of the dark theater and make out the entire time."

"Or we could go home and get some sleep, since we both have to work in the morning."

"That's not nearly as much fun." He took her hand, pulling her toward the door. "Come on. Let's go find some trouble."

"I'm not the trouble type," she said with a laugh, sounding free and happy. It made him want to sweep her into his arms and never let go.

When she made a feeble attempt to pull away, he slipped his arms around her waist, picking her up and carrying her toward where his truck was parked on the other side of the street. She pretended to fight him, her laughter warming his heart. He set her on her feet in the middle of the road, then slowly lowered his lips to hers, gently brushing them with his own before releasing her.

She fisted the front of his shirt, yanking him closer, surprising him. "No, no. You don't get to be a tease like that."

"I thought you like it when I tease," he murmured.

"I do. But I also like this." She kissed him slowly and deeply right there in the middle of Main Street.

A truck rumbled by, its horn tooting cheerfully. Myles continued to kiss her, loving that he had been wrong about Karen Hartley and her ability to consider him as someone worthy of her time, and possibly even her heart.

hings were happening. And not just the Thursday night double date. Go figure that Jackie had managed to make that happen for the four of them despite Karen's protests.

The fundraiser was coming together with astonishing speed, making Karen giddy. The community's immediate support was astonishing, and she had a feeling a lot of it had to do with Myles Cameron Wylder.

Was there a reason for him to be so invested in the library other than any feelings he might have for her? He wasn't a big reader, which made her believe that maybe Myles was truly interested.

That idea was both terrifying and thrilling.

And the best part yet was that tonight the two of them were part of a double date.

Jackie parked her sports car in the country club parking lot and Karen climbed out, humming to herself.

Ryan popped out of his truck, nodding to them.

"Where's Myles?" she asked, her good mood crashing at the thought that he might have bailed.

"He's inside." Ryan waved his phone. "I had to make a call. It sounds like the ranch next to ours just got purchased in a private sale." He shook his head and muttered something Karen couldn't hear.

"You look handsome tonight," Jackie said, tipping her head to look at Ryan through her lashes.

"Why didn't they tell us they wanted to sell? I had an idea." Ryan appeared miffed.

Ignoring Jackie, he looked Karen over from her lightly curled hair down to her pretty sandals, taking in her expression before frowning at her fitted cotton sundress with its modest square neckline.

"What?" Karen asked.

"You seem different. Happier, I think."

"It's because she loves golf now," Jackie teased. "She's excited to get a chance to rub in her recent win by waving around the gift certificate."

Karen laughed. "Am not!" She turned to Ryan, slightly amused by his pointed remark about her appearance. "And I am happy tonight. I suppose that's what's different about me." She frowned, wondering if that meant she seemed unhappy most of the time, or if her excitement over being out with Myles was showing more than she'd expected it to.

"She's gorgeous, Ryan," Jackie said, hooking her arm through Karen's in support. "It wouldn't kill you to learn how to compliment a woman. She won't automatically latch on to you and insist you marry her, you know."

"Things going well with the fundraiser?" he asked, giving Jackie a weird look.

"Very much so. Myles has been amazing." Karen mentally winced. Even she could hear the affection in her voice when she said his name.

"He's the kind of man who acts when you need him to. He'd jump into a raging river to save you without even a flicker of hesitation." There was weight behind Ryan's words and Karen remained silent to hear what else he might reveal about the man she was falling for. "He's good at taking action."

"That's the dream," Jackie said quietly, nudging Karen as they moved toward the country club.

"He's a good person to have on your team. A good assistant," Ryan stated, then cleared his throat. "Just don't take that as a reason to run off and elope."

Karen let out an embarrassed laugh. Elope? They were nowhere near that kind of commitment. This was their first date, and it was a double date at that. Marriage of any form was not on the horizon.

"Why not? That would be incredibly romantic." Jackie came to a stop, hands on her hips as she confronted Ryan.

"Marriage is always a bad decision. And eloping is like a bad decision on steroids." He gave her a big, fake smile.

She shook her head. "You need to get a life, my friend."

"It's a thing, okay?" His expression turned stormy in that way Myles's sometimes did.

"Fine, it's a thing," Jackie said, rolling her eyes. "Like anyone would ever want to elope with you," she muttered. "Old Man Lovely won't ever have to worry about you appearing on his chapel doorstep on New Year's Eve."

Karen bit back her amusement at Jackie's dig. She was right, Grant Lovely, a man with the authority to circumvent current Texas marriage laws and perform shotgun weddings wasn't likely to ever have to worry about facing Ryan.

A dark silence settled in between Jackie and Ryan as they continued toward the clubhouse.

"You two are close, aren't you? You and Myles?" Karen asked Ryan, trying to shift gears so the two didn't ruin supper.

"Myles and I complement each other," he said, shooting Jackie an angry look.

She stuck her tongue out at him and hooked her arm through

Karen's again. "Just like the two of you do," she said kindly, refer-ring to Karen and Myles.

"I'm the thinker, he's the doer," Ryan said, opening the club-house door.

"You know, speaking of doing..." Jackie paused dramatically. "I heard there were two people kissing in the middle of Main Street last night. Did you hear that, Ryan?"

Karen exhaled, eyes closed. She'd known that was going to come up at some point. She'd already heard it from students and teachers alike at school.

"Wonder who that might have been," Myles said, joining them just inside the doors. He slid a hand along Karen's lower back, placing a kiss on her cheek in a slow, deliberate way that made her feel special.

"Does that mean you're considering retracting your I-don't-date-cowboys rule?" Jackie asked Karen.

"I can play up the football coach angle if that's more your speed. But I didn't think you were into jocks." Myles was watching her, his finger trailing lazily up her bare arm. All she could think was that everything about Myles was her speed these days. "By the way, you look beautiful tonight."

"That's because there are no buttons for her to do up to her chin," Jackie said, giving her a teasing nudge.

"Maybe that's it." Myles's eyes were locked on Karen's and she had a feeling he was barely registering anything else. She felt the same way.

"Maybe it's because I'm happy," she said quietly.

"Why's that?"

A shy smile stole its way out of lockdown. "I get to have dinner with a very handsome, smart man tonight."

"And he's hungry," Ryan said. "Are we going to sit down or what?"

Jackie giggled. "Come on, Ryan. I think it'll be on us to hold up the dinner conversation."

Myles took Karen by the hand, whispering in her ear, "Have I ever mentioned how sexy I find librarians?"

"No," she breathed, checking his beautiful blue eyes to see if what he was saying was true.

It was.

"I do. Especially this one."

She blushed, trying to focus on where she was putting her feet as they weaved their way among the tables.

"And what's so sexy about me?" she asked, hoping he mentioned something other than her bra size.

"You make difficult things seem easy."

"I do?"

"You're smart, kind and real."

"Real?" They were at their table and she paused as he pulled a chair out for her. Did he mean her hair, nails and boobs? She was very unlike his former girlfriends in those regards.

"Yeah."

"I'm bookish."

"I like bookish."

"But you're not a big reader?"

"It doesn't mean I don't wish that I was."

"That's easy to fix." She eyed him, testing her theory that there was more behind Myles and his aversion to being bookish. If it was an image thing she figured he'd just keep an interest in reading quiet, and not draw attention to it. If it was more, he'd tell her.

"Is it?" His gaze was locked on her mouth and she wondered if he was going to kiss her in the middle of the restaurant. She had a feeling she wouldn't mind.

"Yeah." She gave him a playful smile. "Just read more."

He returned the smile with a sadness that made her rewind what she'd said as he pushed her chair closer to the table for her.

It wasn't an image thing, was it? He wasn't illiterate—he was taking a course. So what was it? A learning disability?

104

"If you want to be bookish... just read." She watched him, and caught Jackie and Ryan exchange a glance.

Ryan said, opening his menu, "Myles has never been a huge reader."

"Is it a deal breaker if I don't get into books as much as you do?" Myles asked. His tone was light, but the atmosphere had changed and it felt as though her response mattered more than he would ever admit. She felt a sudden heat, a pressure to say the right thing, to figure out the reasoning behind his reading aversion.

She placed her hand over Myles's. Whether or not her boyfriend was a bookworm didn't seem to matter nearly as much to her as it once had. Myles had made her realize that sometimes spending time with people who were different only made them and the world around her all the more interesting.

And it opened doors in her thinking and her everyday life, too. She knew Myles was the one who'd pushed the school into bringing her on as a cheer manager and she was good at it, adding a new dimension to the team as well as her own life. And look at her and golf! For the first time she looked forward to participating in a sport.

Karen shrugged, unsure how to express her change of heart without sounding sappy or insincere. "Because I love books, I've always just kind of imagined myself with someone who shares that love, challenges me intellectually, and I—"

"Can I take your drink orders?" A waiter appeared between her and Myles.

"A bottle of house red," Ryan said. He lifted his brows to confirm the selection, and everyone nodded.

"And a round of water," Jackie added.

"I admire that you've put so much time and effort into helping the library," Karen said to Myles after the waiter left. Her train of thought derailed, she wasn't able to get back to what she had planned to say, and felt as though she'd left something hanging in the air, unresolved and unexpressed. But before she could figure out how to recover, the conversation moved on, leaving the subject behind.

JACKIE HAD WRANGLED it so the brothers were split up for the drive home, Ryan riding with Jackie—she'd promised he could drive her sports car—and Myles giving Karen a ride home in Ryan's Jeep.

In her driveway, Karen had given him a resolve-weakening kiss. Myles wasn't sure exactly which resolve was being weakened, but he was fairly confident it was that one where he resisted the urge to throw her over his shoulder and claim her as his soul mate or some such thing.

The problem was, he was never going to magically become the type to sit in a wing-backed chair smoking a pipe, reading glasses perched on the end of his nose, pondering dusty old tomes written by some long-dead men. That made him wonder if he was just an itch she was looking to scratch, because he was always going to be a man who liked to work with his hands and be involved in sports as well as ranching.

The problem was, he was already thinking beyond next week and beyond the fundraiser. A lot further beyond. He could see Karen's bright and sunny laughter, her serious rule-following side lighting up his life and keeping him in line for years to come.

Could she handle that?

She had agreed to work with him, had let him kiss her in the middle of the street without later dying of mortification when teased about it, and she'd willingly come on tonight's double date. Surely she wasn't the type to string a man along. And yet he felt as though he needed to solidify himself as something real in her life. Someone worthy of serious consideration. Something more than an itch to scratch or a box to check off on her young-and-single bucket list.

Maybe he should read *The Da Vinci Code* so they could discuss it at length.

He sighed. It would be easier to write a poem. They were short, didn't have to make complete sense, and he could just pour whatever was in his head into some weird, possibly rhyming format.

Yeah, a poem would speak her language. And he knew just who to call upon for help.

Myles parked his truck behind Call of the Wyld(er) located just behind The Watering Hole tavern.

"Brant!" Myles yelled through the back door to the clinic. He waited for a reply. "The lights are on. I know you're here because you believe in conserving energy like a good person."

He walked through the back storage area with an eye out for his brother.

"Why did I ever give you the code to the back door?" Brant called from the surgery.

Myles headed left and found his brother and April MacFarlane poring over papers laid out on a stainless steel gurney.

"Because you needed my help building that wonderful apartment you live in upstairs." That project had almost convinced him to leave the ranch and take up construction. It had been fun, proving to himself that he had untapped skills. However, all the codes and rules had squelched the enjoyment out of doing it every day.

"Hey, April. How's it going?" He looked around for her son. "Where's your little guy?"

"At home. I was in town visiting your mom and saw the lights on in here." She shuffled the papers they'd been looking at into a pile and tugged at her shirt, which was a little snug and didn't seem to want to stay how she adjusted it.

"What have you got going on?" He came over to take a peek, but she tucked them into a folder.

"It's a secret." She gave him a sweet smile.

He rolled his eyes. April was like Brant, kind and quiet, but with lots going on under the surface, which made them excellent secret keepers. He knew from past experience there was no point in trying to get them to reveal whatever it was they had been working on until they were ready.

It was really annoying.

"I'll give you my waterfall," Myles said, reverting to the familiar barter system they'd once had as kids back on the ranch.

"I'm over those so-called waterfalls. I've been out of Texas now and know what a real waterfall looks like."

"What? That brown water rushing over rocks doesn't count as real?"

"Not even as rapids."

Myles pretended he'd been shot in the heart and staggered, his cowboy boots slipping on the floor, adding to his drama.

April laughed. "Don't kill yourself."

Myles dropped his act, wishing her son had been there to witness it. Kurt would have thought he was hilarious.

April placed a hand on Brant's right cheek, giving him a light kiss on the other. "Thanks for your help."

"Hey, why don't I ever get a kiss on the cheek?" Myles asked.

"Because you'd aim for the mouth."

"Am I ever going to live that down? I was thirteen!"

She smirked and spun in her boots, giving the brothers a little wave, the light dancing off the fake gems attached to the rear pockets of her jeans. "See y'all on the flip side."

"Bye, April."

"I'll lock it on my way out," she called, disappearing into the clinic's front area.

"She has a key?"

"I hired her to help out here and there."

"That's a long drive from Riverbend."

"It's just casual."

"The work or your relationship? She's married, you know." She'd found herself in enough of a mess getting involved with the Wylders in the past. She didn't need Brant messing things up for her, especially if she and Heath were working through a tough patch in their marriage.

"You don't have to preach ethics to me," Brant said, and Myles relaxed. That much was true. If any of the Wylders were to stick to the straight and narrow, it would be the middle brother.

The bell on the front door rang faintly as April left.

"You know, for all the kids who could've ended up living on the ranch growing up," Myles said, "she wasn't too bad."

"So what's up?" Brant asked, arms crossed. He was wearing a white surgical coat and a small, drowsy looking dog lay in a nearby kennel.

"Is that Mrs. Fisher's dog?"

Brant nodded. "He had a run-in with Bill."

"The armadillo?"

"Yep. I don't recommend taking him on. He bites and scratches."

It took Myles a moment to remember why he'd come to see his brother. "You're good with words."

Brant took a moment to size him up before saying, "I'm not writing love letters to Karen for you."

Seriously? How had he come to that conclusion so quickly?

Myles held out his hands, shooting him an offended look. "I could write love letters in my sleep."

Brant tipped his head to the side and narrowed one eye.

"Okay, okay." Yeah, he'd come to his brother for this stuff before. And yeah, it had backfired in high school with Daisy-Mae, who hadn't understood what he'd been trying to say. Backfired again in his twenties with Jackie, who had laughed sweetly, then clued him in about how she wasn't actually interested in *him*. That had hurt. He'd thought her flirting was for real.

"I come up with the words and the feelings or whatever," Myles said to Brant, "and you just put them down in a way that makes actual sense to other human beings."

"I'm your scribe?"

"Yeah, sure. Karen likes word nerds." He shrugged.

"It won't work."

"Why not?"

"Cyrano."

"Who?"

"You're fixin' to lie to her. Deceive her. Pretend to be someone you aren't."

"Good thing I'm not planning to do any of those things."

"She's going to fall in love with me, not you."

"Excuse me?" Blood rushed in Myles's ears and he stepped closer.

Brant raised his hands as though expecting to be hit. "If the poem comes from me, she falls for me. Not you."

"Just write down the stuff I say in a way that'll make sense."

He didn't budge.

"Do I have to ask Ryan? Because if I go to him I'll never hear the end of it." Myles threw himself into one of the rolling chairs and skidded across the room.

Brant leaned against the gurney, watching him. "You really like her, don't you?"

"She's all I think about." Frustrated with how far into his soul she'd gotten in such a short time, Myles chopped the air with a hand. "I'll be coaching on the field, and suddenly I'll find myself watching her with the cheerleaders, the game completely forgotten. I almost got hit by two players on the sidelines the other day. I felt like a moron."

"You're in love."

"It's not love. It's just highly intense feelings of attraction."

"Shall I write that down in your poem? I'm sure that'll win her over."

"You'll help?" Myles dug into the floor with the heels of his boots, pulling himself closer to his older brother. "Really?"

Brant was trustworthy, especially with something like this, and sensitive enough to not tease him too much. In all their years, he'd never once given up Myles's secret, never once given him an I-told-you-so when his poems had failed to hit their mark.

Brant moved to the built-in desk along the far wall. He opened his laptop, then, changing his mind, pulled a pad of paper from a drawer. "Don't say anything disgusting, because I can't afford a lobotomy when the brain scrub doesn't work. In other words, don't say anything I can't unhear."

That was fair. Myles admitted he'd gone a little far with the poem for Daisy-Mae in high school, but he'd also overheard his brother using one of his lines on a gal who'd later become a girl-friend for several years.

"Am I safe to talk about the buttons on her shirt, and how her kisses taste like honey?"

Brant had picked up a pen, but threw it down on a nearby stainless steel instrument tray with fake disgust. "I'm out."

Myles laughed. "You're my favorite brother, you know that?"

"One false move and I take back my help."

"One day you're going to find a woman who makes you feel like this. Then you'll come to me for ideas." He rubbed his hands together. "I tell you, the two of us could put Hallmark out of business."

Brant sighed and picked up the pen again. "Well?"

Myles jerked in surprise. "Oh. We're doing this right now? Okay…" Beside him a rodeo queen jean jacket rested on a chair. "What was April doing here, by the way?"

"I see we're going to be here all night. Should we go to the diner and stock up on coffee?"

"No, I've got this. I have an early day tomorrow as well as a football game." Myles shut his eyes, focusing on Karen and what he wanted to say to her, what he wanted to lay at her feet to prove that he was worthy of her—all of her.

KAREN STILL HAD a ton of things to do tonight and she couldn't seem to get the floppy bag of cheerleader pompoms, megaphones and other special game props into the trunk of her car without the other end flopping right back out again. Where was Myles when she needed him? They hadn't crossed paths since last night's double date, and when she'd texted him that morning to see if he'd swing by the school at lunch to check over the event tickets for errors, he'd texted back a slightly incoherent reply. She got that he wasn't a big book nerd like she was, but where was his care for basic grammar and rules of punctuation? Why didn't people check over their dictated messages before sending? The world was going to you-know-where in a hand basket.

Luckily, Ryan had been in the staff room and hadn't minded peeking at the tickets, finding a homophone error that would have caused her great embarrassment.

As Karen struggled with the awkward bag she worried that Myles might have changed his mind about working with her after the date. Every time she'd looked his way during the game tonight she'd caught sight of Jackie, who had ensconced herself at the sidelines, helping refill water containers for the football players, cheerleaders and even Karen. At one point she'd been taking player statistics. And every time she caught Karen's eye she'd make a heart shape with her hands, smile and look over at Myles.

Where was he, anyway? He'd said he'd meet her at her car after the game. Was he going to ditch on her? She couldn't pull off the fundraiser without him. It had gone against her better judgment to agree to his help in the first place. The man didn't even keep a written list, preferring to remember everything, an entirely fallible system.

And what was up with her head cheerleader? Robyn was acting like cheer was a form of torture, when she used to live for the sport. If she wasn't on her game, the whole routine would fall apart, and there went their chance to win a competition in San Antonio in a few weeks.

Karen grumbled as the bag began to sag out of her trunk again, then jumped when Myles appeared at her elbow, shoving it in with his big hands.

"Thank you! I was starting to think you weren't going to show up," she said, slamming the trunk lid quickly. She turned and looked at him curiously under the parking lot lights.

She'd seen him shouting at the players from the sidelines during tonight's game, more intense than usual. He tended to run alongside the play, calling instructions or encouragement, and tonight had been no different in that regard, despite the absence of sneakers and track pants, his usual coaching wardrobe. In fact, he was a sweaty mess, his T-shirt stuck to his broad chest. How had he managed to keep up with the players while wearing cowboy boots and jeans?

He shifted, looking almost shy, and as though he might be hiding something.

"What's up? What's wrong?" *Please don't bail on me.*

"Nothing. Everything's fine."

He hadn't kissed her hello, and she wasn't sure if she should lean in for one. What if he left her hanging? She'd look like an idiot to anyone in the parking lot. They had kissed on Main Street, but that had been two days ago, which she knew was a lifetime in the universe of Myles Wylder. He had been careful to keep their attraction low-key around the school, and now she was wondering if it had been for her benefit or for his. Then again, they'd only been kissing since Sunday and it was now

Friday night. It hadn't even been a week and she was all twisted up about him.

Karen told herself to get a grip. She was stressed out from doing so much, and he likely felt the same way. Her insecurity was unjustified, as was her fear of being rejected. The man had a life, too, and had put a lot on hold to help her.

She pulled in a deep, calming breath. "I sent the tickets for both the fair and the dinner dance to be printed."

"Great."

"Seriously." She moved around to the front of the car to be closer to where he'd drifted to, and placed her hands on its cool hood. "What's up?"

The Torpedoes had won by a wide margin tonight, bringing them one game closer to a spot in the bi-district playoffs the week after next. Karen had seen Myles after several wins and losses, and he was never like this. Was he having doubts about them pulling off the fair? Had the weather forecast changed and they'd find themselves rained out? Should she be starting the new job search as well as looking into breaking her housing lease?

"Was Davis going on again about how he wants his boy to go to State?" she asked tentatively. The local DJ really got into the game, sometimes giving the coaches and officials a hard time about what was going on out on the field, and getting ejected as a result. The man wanted the state championship trophy more than anyone she knew. And there were a lot of people who wanted it. Badly.

"I have something for you." Myles reached into the back pocket of his jeans, pulled out a folded piece of paper and handed it to her.

"Why are you wearing jeans?"

"I forgot to change."

She almost gave an amused laugh before realizing he was serious. What was going on with this man?

She had begun to unfold the paper without looking at it, and she glanced away from Myles to peek at the typed words that ran in a narrow column down the middle. "What's this?" She tilted the page toward a streetlight and began skimming the lines, realizing it was a poem entitled "Kitty." Karen jerked her head up, visually confirming with Myles that she really was reading a poem written for her, and not for a cat that wore button-up shirts.

Myles swallowed hard and licked his lips, his eyes darting, his hands sliding down the thighs of his jeans before settling into his back pockets. He couldn't seem to stay still. The charming, debonair Myles Wylder was literally jumping out of his skin.

Karen started at the beginning again, reading the poem slowly. It was about her eyes, her shirt buttons, her serious demeanor and sexy glasses.

She didn't know what to do. She had never had anyone write a poem about her before. And from the way she was described, she could tell that the author cared a great deal about her, the subject. Her everyday traits seemed sensual and sexy. The poem expressed exactly how Myles made *her* feel when he looked at her.

He had written this. He was not illiterate. In fact, she was darn sure there was not a thing wrong with Myles Wylder other than a fear of appearing bookish and uncool, and he had temporarily set that aside by putting his thoughts on paper. For her.

Wordlessly, she finished the poem, then slowly slid her arms around Myles's back, holding him close and wondering why she had ever overlooked cowboys.

8

*M*yles felt as though his feet barely touched the ground as he moved across the parking lot to his truck. Karen had liked his poem, and he could tell it had struck exactly the right note. The fact that Brant had helped him type it up and organize his thoughts didn't matter. The heart and soul of the poem had been all him, and Karen had loved every word.

He might not be able to read a book with the ease and speed that she could, but he could speak her language and make her happy.

He turned back to where Karen was sitting in her car, windows down.

"You know you're going to need a dress for the dance?" he called.

"I have one." She leaned an elbow on the frame of the car door, her eyes still sparkling from the poem and the kisses that had followed before they started getting catcalls from football players and fans leaving the area.

"Does it have buttons?" he asked, returning to her car.

She started to speak, then closed her mouth.

He opened her door and held out his hand. "Come on,

tonight's game was an early one. I betcha the mall is still open in San Antonio." They would spend more time driving there than in the stores, probably, but the woman had worked so hard on this event she deserved to look gorgeous for it.

"There are other things we should be doing to get ready," she said, even though she placed her hand in his. "And we won't get there before closing."

"I'll drive fast." He caught her look. "Okay, I'll stay close to the speed limit."

"Myles!"

"The mall I'm thinking of is open late tonight."

"How do you know?"

"According to the radio there's a pre-pre-Black Friday event going on, which means we have until midnight."

"I don't know..."

"You've been working hard all week, and you deserve some fun. We'll stop at the diner and get milkshakes to go, listen to loud music and let our hair down for a few hours. We can get all the stuff on your list done tomorrow."

She was obviously considering. "And what are you going to wear to the dance?"

He shrugged. "I'm a dude. It doesn't matter."

She tipped her chin upward. "Maybe it matters to me."

"I'll wear what I wore to the last barn dance."

Karen narrowed her eyes as she followed him toward his truck, after rolling up the windows and locking her car. In Sweetheart Creek it would be safe, the only concern being that someone might worry about her if the vehicle was left for too long.

"What was with that outfit, anyway?" Karen asked.

"Just felt like doing something different."

"To get my attention?" she asked. He didn't reply. "You did look handsome."

117

"Why do I feel as though you're going to add 'but' to the end of that compliment?"

"There isn't one."

"There is." He could feel it.

"But nothing. I'm starting to gain a fondness for cowboys, that's all."

He felt a smile crack his face. "Then I know exactly what to wear."

"What?"

"A surprise."

She was about to climb into his truck, but stopped, hand on the door handle. "Maybe I should go shopping with Jackie and Laura then."

"Why?"

"If I can't see your outfit before the dance, then why should you see mine?"

"When else are you going to have time?"

The event was in eight days, and he knew how busy she would be until then, between work and last-minutes details. There was no chance she was going to make it to San Antonio, and Jenny's shop, Blue Tumbleweed, which specialized in Western wear, wasn't likely to have something quite to Karen's tastes for an event like this.

She was gazing out over the emptying parking lot, a thoughtful look on her face. "I considered your plan," she said after a moment.

"And?"

"It's sound."

Myles didn't ask again, just drove them to the diner, where he collected two milkshakes as promised, as well as a lot of chatter about that night's game and the upcoming fair, before they continued on to the city.

He parked outside the mall, then followed Karen inside. She

took his hand as they entered, and he had that walking-on-air sensation again. This could work between them. Really work.

"If we have time, we can stop at the bookstore," she said, smiling, walking backward for a step or two, her hand firmly in his.

"You don't get enough of books at work?" he asked in wonder. Members of his family enjoyed reading, but he'd never met anyone quite as in love with books as Karen. But he supposed that was what made her good at her job.

"There's no such thing as enough books," she said happily.

"How many do you have at home?"

"Oh, I don't know," she replied, leading him toward a store. "A couple hundred? A thousand? Are we counting digital or just paperback and hardcover?"

Myles laughed. "Never mind. How about I ask if you can make it to your bed, or if you have to run a book gauntlet to get there?"

"And why would you care about something like that?" She gave him a teasing smile that sent a shower of sparks up his spine.

"No reason."

"Here we are. Wait out here. I'll just be a few minutes."

The few times he'd ended up shopping with Jackie, April or his mother it had never been just a few minutes. Not unless that was code for "give me an hour."

Myles sat in an armchair in the main aisle of the mall, his mind drifting before he figured he should analyze the night's football game. Something was still up with their quarterback Hernandez, but for whatever reason he could barely recall the details of the game to sort out what was off. Where had his mind been for those two hours?

Karen. It had been on Karen and the folded poem in his back pocket. Before he had a chance to dive further into his thoughts, Karen popped out of the store, shopping bag in hand.

"For real?" he asked.

"I think you'll like it." She hustled over to a shoe store and shook her head at the window display. "I think I have something that'll work." Next door was a lingerie boutique. "But I do need to stop in here."

"If you need an opinion or a sizing expert," he said, stepping forward, "I'd be happy to help."

She laughed. "I'm sure you would." She placed a hand on his chest as though holding him back. "But no."

He acted crestfallen and she pulled him into her arms, giving him the hottest kiss he'd ever had in public.

Best rejection ever.

EXCITED to have a pretty dress to wear to the fundraiser dance, Karen pulled Myles into her favorite bookstore. In the doorway she paused for a second to inhale the scent of new books. It seemed every time she came in here the gift section had expanded, nudging out books. She supposed it made sense with digital books becoming more popular, but it made her heart ache to see the choices continue to dwindle.

She headed to the book club section near the back and scanned the display table. She had read most of the choices, but picked up two she'd heard about from patrons or online.

Myles took her shopping bag, as well as the books, to free her hands. She shot him a grateful smile, then headed to the sports section. Knowing most of her male patrons at the library, young and old, preferred nonfiction, she figured Myles would be the same, especially with his take-charge persona. Now that she realized he had a natural ability with the written word, she knew for sure that all he needed was the right book and her world of reading would open up for him as well.

"On the radio I heard of this memoir about a Texas football coach. Apparently it's really good. Have you read it yet?"

Myles shook his head.

She skimmed the shelves, found the book and held it up.

"He looks familiar," Myles said.

"When I heard about it, I thought of you." She added the copy to her pile.

"I'm still working on *The Da Vinci Code*," Myles said, handing it back to her.

"My treat." If he was anything like her, and she was starting to believe he was, he might want something new for when he was done, and this book could be the ticket, a story he could identify with. She slipped it back onto the stack in his arms.

"You might like this one, too." She held out a book. "Have you read it?"

"Nope." Myles shifted, looking ill at ease. She thought of how he'd fought her for their supper bill at the diner the other night and how he'd insisted on paying for her milkshake tonight.

"Seriously, my treat. I have piles of gift certificates and reward points here." New books were one of her few splurges, and the idea of sharing the treat with Myles made it all the more fun. "Plus I think I owe you a book from that bet on the golf course."

"I'm not sure we ever established who owes who."

"This looks amusing." She flipped through a book on life according to golfers.

An announcement over the speaker warned that the store was closing in five minutes.

"We could share this one." Karen handed it to Myles. "Read the back cover to me while I keep looking."

"I don't need this many books."

"Just read the blurb and see if it suits you. Oh, and this one, too." There was nothing as exciting as new books. You never knew what journey they would take you on.

Myles shifted his arm so she couldn't add the book to his stack.

"What?" There was a stubborn set to his jaw she hadn't seen before. "Really, I have *tons* of gift cards from family and friends."

"I read maybe a book a year. If you add any more, it'll take me forever. I'm not a reader, Karen."

She looked at the pile in his arms, confused. How could a man who wrote such beautiful poems read only one book a year? He was studying the football textbook right now, as well as reading *The Da Vinci Code*. That was two, and surely he'd want something once he was finished, even if that was a month or two down the road.

If he got through only a book a year did that mean he wasn't really reading the one she'd given him, and she'd fallen for his pickup lines? That didn't feel right. And neither did his insistence about not being a reader. But there was something there. Something she hadn't quite figured out yet.

Knowing she should back off, but unable to leave the mystery of Myles and his aversion to reading alone, she quirked her head, watching him as she asked, "What was it you said to me when I said I sucked at golf? I thought I wasn't sporty or athletic, and you showed me I was wrong."

"I appreciate your generosity," Myles said, his tone gentle. He was standing comfortably close, running a hand up and down her arm in a soothing motion. "But I'm never going to be the big reader you are."

There was a disturbing remorsefulness to his expression that made her feel as though he wouldn't even want to try and meet her halfway—that it was all or nothing. It felt like he was letting her down easy or breaking up with her.

Mortified that she'd misread him and the situation, and desperate to leave in case she started crying, she snatched the stack of books from him. She selected the bottom one and deposited the rest on a nearby cart. "Let's go."

"Karen," Myles said, catching her arm as she moved away.

"No, it's fine." She kept walking, shaking him off. "I don't like people claiming my free time or making assumptions about me, and I just did that to you. I'm sorry. I won't do it again."

She felt Myles fall back as she all but ran toward the cashier. As they left the store, she took her shopping bags from him, clutching her new book to her chest.

She'd worked hard playing golf with him so as not to let him down, but he refused to read a silly book about life rules according to golfers?

Why was he so adamant about not reading? And why was she so adamant that he become a book nerd like her? Didn't she like him for who he was—no changes required?

But the poem? Had it simply been part of his quest to win her over, to make her think they were more alike than they were? That didn't add up, either.

"I'm sorry I don't read as much," he said, keeping pace with her, "or as quickly as you do."

"That's a stupid thing to apologize for." This whole fight was ridiculous and confusing.

They were silent all the way across the parking lot. As Myles started his truck, he said, "I don't sit down a lot, and I lose track of the beginning of the book by the time I get to the end." He looked uncomfortable, his gaze avoiding her.

"Try audiobooks," she said automatically. She wasn't sure why she was so upset, but it felt as though somewhere along the line he hadn't been totally upfront about who he was, and his rejection in the store had felt personal.

Maybe she'd been right when she'd assumed he was a man she'd be wise to avoid. She'd gotten herself muddled up with him because of his kisses. And honestly, maybe they weren't that amazing. Maybe they just felt sexy because he knew what he was doing, and it didn't feel as though he was doing math equations in his head to stay focused on her lips.

"You can borrow audiobooks from the library and listen to them on your smart phone. They aren't as expensive as they used to be," she said, kicking into librarian mode. Anything to get a book in someone's hands, even a guy who wasn't particularly interested.

Would she ever learn? He obviously didn't share her passion for books, and despite her attempts, he refused to engage, even while being on board to save the library. And somehow, in trying to share her joy, she'd erected a giant wall between herself and this cowboy she'd come to care about.

AFTER GETTING home from the city, where everything had gone spectacularly wrong after he'd refused Karen's gift of more books, Myles frowned at his copy of *The Da Vinci Code*. The book was taunting him from his bedside table, and had each night since she had given it to him. He picked up the hardcover, leafing through the images, reading some of the captions before setting it aside, feeling a headache starting. He rubbed his eyes and picked up his phone. He found the book in digital audiobook format, purchased it, then had the device begin reading it out loud.

With Buckey curled up on her dog bed nearby, Myles stretched out with his headphones on, determined to get through the story and channel at least a little of the book nerd Karen so obviously was seeking from him.

He woke up early the next morning, the book nearly finished, his headphones still on. Audiobooks weren't the ticket, either, apparently. He shut off the device and stumbled into the kitchen, hoping for breakfast even though it wasn't yet six o'clock. Around now his mother usually walked over from the tiny house she'd had moved into the yard when she'd moved back from town. She said she preferred to come and cook in a "real kitchen."

Buckey followed him into the sunny room, her claws clacking

on the tile floor, nose snuffling the air. Myles did the same. No breakfast. No coffee.

He dropped a scoop of kibble into Buckey's dish and whistled for Levi's dog in case he hadn't been fed yet. When Lupe didn't come, Myles checked the cow-shaped clock on the wall, figuring he'd missed Levi and his dog by about fifteen minutes. His brother could be out having coffee at the fence with Laura, although the coffeepot was empty and Myles hadn't noted her car in the driveway when he'd looked out the front window earlier. And with the sun not due to rise for a while yet, Myles figured the eldest Wylder brother was likely living up to his Type A personality and getting a head start on some chores. Like Myles should, so he could meet up with Karen in time to go over some fundraising details before her shift at the library. It sure would be easier around here if Cole returned to help out.

With a heavy sigh Myles sat at the kitchen table and rubbed his face. Karen had been so excited in the bookstore last night, eagerly filling his arms with books she thought he might like. And then he'd killed that joy with a few quick words.

What was wrong with him? Why couldn't he just tell her the truth and trust her not to change her opinion of him? But it killed him to think she might see the parts of himself he'd tried to hide, the parts that might separate them in ways he didn't want to ever have to handle.

But he'd been kidding himself with the thought that making her smile was worth more than her passion for books or how she perceived intelligence based on an ability to read like the wind. To her, catching a football or being able to lasso a calf on the first try meant nothing, and it felt like that was all he had.

"Good morning, sunshine," his mother said, giving him a little pat on the back as she hurried into the kitchen. She was wearing her going-to-town boots, and looked freshly showered, bright-eyed and happy.

"Where are you off to?" he asked.

Buckey had finished gobbling her food and was standing at the sliding door, ready to go out for the day. Myles reached over from his spot at the long table and pushed it open for her, then inhaled the morning air. It was going to be a gorgeous day and he hoped the weather held for their fair next weekend.

Carmichael hustled in from his own house on the property and, after giving Maria an appraising look, asked, "Where's breakfast? You fixin' somethin' before you go to town?"

"I have to get my car's air filter swapped out at Clint's," Maria said to Myles. To her father-in-law she said, "I'll make breakfast first."

"Good." The man, approaching eighty, eased into the chair and crossed his arms. "I'm going to need a coffee, too."

"You know how the machine works." She gave him a pointed look and he grumbled, getting up again.

"You'd think age mattered for something around here."

"Clint's open on Saturdays now?" Myles asked.

"I tried to get it done yesterday, but he was out for lunch." She wiped her hands on the apron she'd wrapped around her waist, then began furiously whisking pancake batter. "He told me to pop by today."

"Is changing the filter all he's doing?" Myles asked wryly. It felt odd teasing his mother about a man who wasn't his father, but she was free to date, and his dad had already remarried.

"That is all," Maria said sternly, but her cheeks flushed.

"I thought Levi changed your air filter a few weeks ago," Carmichael stated, his eyes narrowed as though he was sniffing out an inconsistency in her story.

"He ordered the wrong size. Clint has the right one, and said it'll only take a jiffy to put in." Maria was bustling around the kitchen with practiced steps. "I may also pop by the library to see if they need help reshelving books, or with some fair preparations."

"Are you taking anyone to the dinner and dance?" Myles asked.

Maria, her back to him, said, "I haven't got my tickets yet. Can I buy them from you?"

"Karen should have them today or tomorrow, I think. How many do you need?"

"Two." She gave him a warning look. "I'm picking one up for Mrs. Fisher, so don't you start."

"Start what? Karen said Mrs. F. will be selling them for us at the diner. Why doesn't she buy hers there?"

"Oh?"

A whisper of doubt entered Myles's mind, but he wasn't sure if he felt his mom was trying to cover up something or if Karen had forgotten to confirm things with Mrs. Fisher. "I'd better double-check. Karen's really good with details, but she's been a bit overwhelmed." He pulled his phone from his jeans pocket, then dictated a message and hit Send.

"So," his mom said, her own voice anything but innocent, "are *you* taking someone?"

"I'll be working at it, Mom—as one of the organizers."

"Make sure you stop and enjoy a dance or two." She had taken a stack of plates from the cupboard, handing them to Myles, who laid them out at the table. "I like Karen. Always have." She passed him a tray of cutlery. "Where's Levi?"

"Getting a head start on chores, I think."

His mother hummed softly to indicate she'd heard him.

"Why?"

"Nothing." She gave a quick smile, making Myles think that she and Levi might also be hiding something, just like Brant and April. Before he could gather more hints to help him figure out what it might be, the front door opened with a shouted "Hello!" A second later Ryan appeared in the kitchen doorway.

"You're here earlier than usual," Maria said to him.

"Heard the stove turn on all the way from town, did ya?" Carmichael asked.

Ryan smiled. "Just like you, only you live right outside the door, so were faster getting here. Save me anything good?"

Carmichael gave a harrumph, but Myles saw the teasing edges of a suppressed smile.

"Hernandez can't do my chores this morning. Robyn has a doctor's appointment. So I thought I'd come early and do Myles's, too."

"Is there snow and ice outside?" Carmichael asked.

"No, dear," Maria said gently, double-checking with a glance out the patio door near the elderly man.

"Okay. 'Cause I was thinking that Satan's homeland may have frozen over with this kid offering to do more than his share around here." He jerked a thumb in Ryan's direction.

Myles let out a bark of laughter, while his brother shook his head in exasperation. "He's trying to save the library, Granddad," Ryan said.

"You sure about the chores?" Myles asked, jumping to his feet. He took a step toward the door, feeling as though he needed to be somewhere, like, right now.

"You were saying during last night's game how much there was to get done, and since I'm here and with nothing to do today..." He gave a shrug.

"Thanks, man." Myles gave his brother a clap on the shoulder on his way to the door.

"Forgetting something?" his mom called from her station at the stove, flipping pancakes.

Myles did an about-face and hurried to her side, then planted a kiss on her cheek. "We missed you when you were living in town, Mom."

She patted his flat stomach. "I know you did."

He laughed and hurried out of the room, knowing exactly where he needed to be.

9

*T*he sun was just streaking the sky when Karen answered her front door.

"Sorry. I hope I didn't wake you," Myles said. His eyes swept over her, no doubt confirming that he had not in fact woken her, seeing as she was dressed and ready for the day ahead. "You said you were an early riser. Have you had breakfast yet?"

"I thought we weren't meeting for another hour or two?"

"Ryan's doing my chores, so I thought we could use the extra time and meet now."

She opened her door a little wider, expecting him to come in.

He shifted on the front walk, taking a step toward his truck parked along the street. "Actually, I was hoping I could take you out for breakfast."

"Take me out?" She wasn't sure if he meant as a date or not. She hadn't slept well last night, tossing and turning, fretting over how sharing her love of books had pretty much bombed with him. This man did not add up with any kind of math she understood.

"There's this little place down the highway. Why don't we sit and eat and take care of some details?"

She hesitated, still trying to sort out what kind of footing they were on—as a couple, or whatever they were. Last night hadn't ended in passionate kisses. And neither of them had apologized, because they hadn't even truly fought. Things were just awkward and weird, and the idea of sitting in The Longhorn Diner to advertise their discomfort to the town didn't hold a lot of appeal. Plus the amount of interruptions about football would make it impossible to hold a conversation, as the team advanced toward State. It was to the point where practically every window in town was plastered with signs supporting the Torpedoes, homes and businesses both.

"Last night you showed me someplace you love. Let me show you somewhere I love."

"I've been to the diner."

"It's not the diner. At least not the one you're thinking of."

"Myles, last night… with me sharing my love of books? It just got awkward and uncomfortable." If they had too many incidents like that, she feared that whatever it was that had been growing between them would dissolve before she got a chance to sort out what kept drawing her to him.

"I know, and I'm sorry. That was my fault for not being upfront with you about me and books."

He wasn't looking at her as he kicked at a piece of loose concrete along her front walk.

She shook her head, unable to figure out what to do with this man. He was going so far out of his way to help with the library, but he was so stubborn about books. "Cowboys confuse me."

He looked up, a question in his sky-blue eyes.

She grabbed her coat, purse and phone. "Why don't you just listen to audiobooks and get over it already?"

"They put me to sleep."

"They put you to sleep?" she repeated.

"Well, last night one did, anyway."

Her heart lifted, letting go of some of the resentment and

confusion she'd been feeling. "You listened to an audiobook last night?"

"You told me to."

"Oh, Myles." She stepped out onto the walk and wrapped her arms around him.

Minutes later they were heading down the highway in his truck, the sun well over the horizon, the dawn shades of orange and pink melted into a blue that matched Myles's eyes.

They pulled into a dirt lot, leaving a cloud of dust floating over the vehicles parked downwind from them. Myles took her hand as he led her toward a small building covered in old hubcaps. Karen winced as the early morning sun struck them, reflecting back a blinding glare. She had no idea what the building underneath looked like or even what color it might be.

"What is this place?"

"A diner."

"This is a restaurant?"

The interior was larger than she'd expected, as the building extended back into the lot. Old fence railings, darkened from years of hands being run over them, marked off sections within the place. The dark wood walls were covered in neon signs, as if the diner doubled as a biker bar at night.

Myles took her to a booth where the plastic cushion on the bench was cracked, but the fabric one at her back was fresh and trendy. The table under her elbows was clean, and a small bouquet of cut flowers in a mason jar sat between them. Most of the decor seemed worn beyond the point of having character, yet other parts of it were bright and new.

Myles waved to a waitress, and gave her what looked like a reversed peace sign, pointing two large fingers down at their table. Karen had brought her notes for the fundraiser, and laid them out, deciding where they should start.

Momentarily, the waitress appeared with coffee and water for them both, then promptly disappeared again.

"How do we get menus around here?" Karen craned her neck, hoping to catch her attention.

"I already ordered."

Karen turned to him. "You ordered for me?"

"I did."

"But how do you know what I like?"

His eyes stayed steady on hers. "You figured you know what books I'd like. I figure I know what food you'd enjoy."

"But you rejected the books."

"You can reject the meal."

Karen rested her hands on the edge of the table and pressed her back into the cushion. She took a moment to breathe and collect her thoughts.

"I can't live without food," Myles said, "and you can't live without books. You showed me something *you* love. Well, now I'm showing you something I love."

Karen's heart sank. He'd rejected what she'd tried to give him last night, and now he'd taken her to a dingy highway diner that he said was dear to him. Was this his way of showing her that a relationship would never work, so she'd wander off on her own instead of him having to break up with her?

She dropped her eyes to her checklist. They just needed to get through this fundraiser and then everything could fall apart.

She was still staring at her list when the waitress set down a heaping plate of food in front of each of them, then a glass jar of ketchup from the pocket of her apron. "Enjoy."

Karen's plate was piled with pancakes, waffles, bacon, scrambled eggs, shredded hash browns, rye toast and two sausage links.

"This is ridiculous. I don't need so much food. There's no way I can get through this."

Myles just gave a shrug and a ghost of a smile. Karen clutched her fork as his words from last night washed over her: *I don't need this many books.*

Was this how he'd felt last night? Was this meal him turning the tables on her so she could feel what he had?

Her voice was weak as she asked, "Is this because I pushed too many books on you last night?"

Myles frowned. "Kitty, this isn't personal. It isn't even about the meal."

"But…" She stared at the food mounded in front of her.

He pointed a fork at her plate. "The best way to know what you like here is to try it all. Just eat what you can and leave the rest."

"And did you do that the first time you came here?"

He grinned. "Yeah, but it turns out I like everything that comes out of that kitchen."

She gave a laugh as he dug into his food with gusto. He wasn't trying to turn the tables on her. Not at all.

Karen was partway through her meal before she realized there was music playing, and the only reason she realized it was live was because it suddenly stopped, and someone began speaking into the sound system. There was a woman at the microphone, reciting what sounded like a poem.

Karen turned to Myles. "This is a poetry slam?"

Was he going to get up onstage and start reciting poems?

"What's a poetry slam?"

Karen shook her head, looking at the woman. The poem had nice imagery, but it wasn't as good as Myles's.

"Have you ever read a poem here?"

"No." He shook his head, an expression of disbelief on his face.

"Why not?"

His eyes locked on hers with that smoldering heat she hadn't seen in hours as he said quietly, "My poems are for one audience and one audience only."

"Oh." She nodded, feeling a sudden need for more air.

Myles was eyeing her sausage. "You going to eat that?"

She shook her head and he reached over with a fork, spearing one of her links.

"How often do you come here?"

"Quite a bit before my mom returned to the ranch. My parents got divorced not that long ago. Mom moved into town and none of us guys are much in the way of cooks."

"So you would come here to eat and listen to poetry?"

"And to the music. No cover songs are allowed, so everything's original. Sometimes it's really bad and sometimes it's really good. I like it when I can catch someone who's heading to Nashville. They're usually pretty good."

"So you're a cowboy who comes here for the poetry and the music? A cowboy who doesn't like having me stack his arms with books?"

Myles laughed. "What can I say? I'm a walking contradiction, Kitty."

"That you are." And somehow that erased all her feelings of doubt from last night, and intrigued her all the more.

KAREN SET down a stack of returned library books on a nearly full reshelving cart. With the phone ringing off the hook about the upcoming fundraiser, as well as having to coordinate their amazing volunteers, she felt as though she was falling further and further behind on her regular tasks, which was something Henry would surely notice and remark upon at the next board meeting.

At least she could work through lunch if she needed to, as Myles's breakfast had filled her to the point of feeling she might never need to eat again.

"Miss Karen, can you read to me?" Faith, a four-year-old with black ringlets that stuck up all over her head, had come around the side of the circulation desk. The girl looked up at her with big brown eyes, clutching a hardcover storybook.

How could she say no? Faith's mom was working on the computer, applying for jobs, and thanks to recent cuts, the children's programmer no longer ran her Saturday morning craft and story time for preschoolers.

Karen looked at her task list before answering. There were more things than she could get through today, and she was supposed to be meeting with Myles again to run through a few items. But if she didn't help patrons, what was the point of saving the library?

The front door opened and Myles entered, shoulders hunched, a large patchwork quilt folded in his arms as he cast his eyes left, then right, as though expecting to be called out on being in the library. He looked like such a typical cowboy in his black hat, his jaw clenched, his blue eyes searching.

"Don't worry," she called to him from behind the computer monitor. "I won't fill your arms with books and insist you read them all."

Myles caught sight of her, the hard lines of his face softening, the tension melting from his shoulders. He came over to the counter.

"I forgot to reply to the text you sent me before breakfast," Karen said quickly, before she forgot. Myles had a way of distracting her. "I am picking up the tickets from Polly after work. And yes, they will be sold at the diner. I confirmed with Mrs. Fisher. She seems a bit distracted, don't you think?"

"Miss Karen, story," Faith whined.

"Just a moment, hon." Without thinking, she accepted the book the little girl held out, and in doing so implicitly agreed to read it. So much for her to-do list.

"I think she's having a tough time with William," Myles said, placing the quilt on the counter, his gaze taking her in, his attention touching briefly on her blouse's short Mao collar, which was fully buttoned. "He hasn't adjusted well to being in a wheelchair."

He patted the beautiful quilt. "This is from Garfield's sister. It's for the silent auction."

"Thanks. She's such an amazing quilter. This will bring in a lot." She carefully set it aside. "Wasn't William's accident quite some time ago?"

Myles nodded.

Jenny Oliver, who was helping with some of the fundraiser tasks, came out of the back room with a stack of discarded library books she'd bound together and decorated as a centerpiece for the fundraiser dinner. She set it on the counter. "For you to inspect before I make more tomorrow."

"These look amazing," Karen said.

Jenny smiled. "Hey, Myles. I didn't think you were into the library scene. It's very nice of you to help out with the library when you don't..." She quickly glanced at Karen, then him again, swallowing hard.

"Yeah, I don't have a lot of free time these days," he replied.

"Right!" she said brightly.

"None of us do," Karen agreed.

Jenny checked her watch. "I've got to run. Blue Tumbleweed opens soon." She disappeared in record time and Faith, still waiting, tugged at Karen's sleeve again.

"Can you read this to the kids?" Karen held the book out to Myles. He was great with teenagers, and she felt confident he could read a quick story to the little ones to get them off her back. "I want to print some stuff off to run past you."

Myles backed away from the circulation desk, hands raised, expression sincere. "I'm sorry. I'd love to, but I have to run. I'm in the middle of moving tables from the community center to the rodeo grounds for the fair." He jerked a thumb over his shoulder, and through the window she could see a truck and a horse trailer out front. "I just wanted to drop off this quilt before it got dirty riding around in the ranch truck. We're still on for meeting again in a few hours?"

"Oh. Okay. Yes, thanks."

"If there's anything else you need me to do today, just let me know."

"We need to look over those papers later. I don't know what's standard in a rental agreement. There's one for the rodeo grounds and one for the community center. Polly said she'd check over the community center one, but I don't want to sign anything until you've read them all."

Myles inhaled as though about to say something, then spotted Faith, who was still waiting, eyes wide and hopeful. He gave her a tip of his hat, then returned his focus to Karen. "Email them to me and I'll scan them. I'm sure they're standard, though. Or when we meet later we can talk them over. Maybe that would be faster."

"Fine," Karen said, rolling her eyes. Cowboys and their aversion to paperwork. Before her job here she'd worked reception at the small medical clinic in Riverbend and had learned that trying to get cowboys to read forms and fill everything out was like pulling teeth. They tended to like to take action, she knew, but sometimes a sit-down to check over the fine print was necessary.

"Miss Karen?" Faith said.

"Of course, Faith. I'm sorry." She stood with the book.

"Faith," called her mother from the computer area, "leave Miss Karen alone. She has work to do."

"It's fine," Karen replied. She called to the other children, who were playing with trains and other toys, or looking at picture books, while their mothers had coffee on the tired-looking couches at the back of the library. "Does anyone else want a story?"

They all scampered to the carpeted area in the front corner, which was decorated with bright colors, children's handprints and plenty of glitter tracked over from the nearby crafting area.

Karen heard a truck engine rev and looked out the front window to where Myles was making his escape. Breakfast had been nice, giving her another insight into the man she was coming to adore. But sometimes, like now, it felt as though they'd hit some sort of invisible barrier, one they kept bumping into when she felt they were getting to know each other at a heart level.

He was still such an enigma. Maybe that was the appeal of cowboys—that mysterious layer they never revealed, so you had to pick and pick, and even after years of being in love you still didn't get all the way through it. Or you got through it only to discover another layer that was even more intriguing.

Karen waited until the children were settled, her heart lifting as they jostled to sit close to her. The children's programmer usually made them back up, but Karen didn't mind having so many little bodies snuggled up to her. It was cozier this way. She opened the book and turned it around so the pages faced the children.

When she finished the book, she closed it and said, "Well, what do you think? Good story?"

They nodded.

"More!" said Tyson, one of the toddlers at the front. He planted his feet, palms on the floor, then slowly rose to a standing position before tearing off to one of the shelves where dinosaur books were displayed. He snatched one and ran back, landing hard in front of her, his fingers getting slammed under the book.

"Are you okay?"

His face crumpled, but he didn't cry. He thrust the book at her. "More. Dinosaurs."

Karen hesitated. If she agreed to one more, then everyone would want to choose a book, too. But if she didn't say yes the sad look on the boy's face would break her heart.

"Okay. Just one more," she said, wriggling as though settling in for a long story. What was half an hour when you were doing something that filled your soul? And if the library closed its doors, what would she remember? Hiding behind her monitor, furiously trying to stay on top of her to-do list, or enjoying a good book with little minds and turning them into readers?

"I'm putting together a fun fair for next weekend. It's going to have lots of games and even a petting zoo. But..." She paused to draw their attention. "It won't happen if I don't get back to working on it after this story. Okay?"

A few of the older children nodded. Tyson patted the dinosaur book's cover with his chubby hand. "More! More dinosaurs!"

"One more it is," she said gently, opening the book. He sat back, satisfied, hands clutched together in his lap.

The kids were all so adorable. She didn't want to allow herself to imagine what a miniature Myles might look like should he choose to have children.

She pushed that thought from her mind, losing herself in the story, making dinosaur grunts and roars as she animated the tale with gestures. The kids giggled, adding their own sounds and causing a ruckus. Karen laughed, delighted that they were turning this quiet space into a place full of life and joy.

As she closed the book, she noticed a few children had risen up onto their knees, heads turned, attention focused on something just inside the main doors. She followed their gazes and saw Brant Wylder with a small dog on a leash.

She didn't think pets were allowed in, but couldn't think of a line in the library manual stating they weren't. While she hesitated, the children swarmed toward Brant's furry friend. He crouched beside the animal, guiding them to pet gently, talking to them calmly as he showed them how to treat the animal. He had that same patience she'd come to admire in his brother Myles.

"Who is this?" Karen asked, setting the dinosaur book back on the display and coming over to see the brown-and-white medium-haired dog.

"This is Ribbons."

"Ribbons is adorable. Is she yours?"

"Her owner passed away, and her extended family doesn't want her. I'm figuring out what she likes and doesn't like so I can find her a suitable home."

Karen felt the story tug at her heartstrings.

"We can take her," Faith said. She raised her voice. "Right, Mommy?"

"We can't afford a dog right now, honey," her mother replied. "She's beautiful, though." She smiled at Brant, then refocused on the computer, no doubt determined to make the most of her daughter's distraction.

"Dogs take a lot of time and money," Brant told the kids. He said to Karen, "I hope it's okay I brought her here. I was trying to think of a place where I could see how well socialized she is."

"Obviously she's good with kids," Karen stated. Ribbons was currently licking Tyson's cheek, and he was giggling, his arms around the dog's neck.

"I think she might have some Cavalier King Charles Spaniel in her," Brant said, gently guiding one of the toddlers' fingers away from Ribbon's eyes, "which means she might bolt if let off leash. But she appears as though she has a lot of other breeds mixed in, so you never know. I've been afraid to check to see if she's a runner."

"Is she house-trained?"

"She's spent the past two nights at my place and has been great."

"Does she like cats?"

"Thinking Ribbons might fit into your life?" Brant asked casually.

"I'm not sure my cats would approve." Karen was trying to recall if they'd ever met a dog.

"I'll take her to the ranch tonight," Brant said, "and let her discover the barn cats. I'll report back on her reaction to them."

What was Karen thinking? She didn't have time for a dog.

What if she ended up moving? Then she'd have to find a place that took both cats and dogs.

Brant's phone rang, and he placed it to his ear while trying to plug the other, still holding on to the leash. The children were chattering loudly, squealing and laughing, totally delighted by Ribbons, who Karen swore was smiling, happy to be the center of attention.

She reached for the leash and shooed Brant away, so he could take what sounded like an important call. The coffee moms were smiling at the scene, offering reprimands to their kids when they looked as if they might be rough with Ribbons.

"Anyone need a dog?" Karen asked.

The women shook their heads. "But she's adorable."

"She is," Karen said, taking in the furry patchwork of brown and white.

"I've got to run," Brant said, getting off the phone. He looked at the dog as though trying to decide what to do. The kids were still swarming around her, trying to get her to lick them, then squealing when she did.

"I want to read Ribbons a story," Faith announced.

Brant winced at Karen, then apologetically asked, "Would it be okay if she stayed here for an hour? I've got an animal emergency with a stuck ewe over on Three Mile Ranch. I'm afraid to take the time to put Ribbons in the kennel at the clinic, and it's too hot to leave her in the truck without putting the windows all the way down." He was angling toward the door, his hand out for the leash despite his request. He was like Myles, careful not to overstep or ask too much. "The ranch I'm going to has some pretty mean dogs who wouldn't think twice about jumping through an open window to defend their territory."

Karen pulled the leash handle to her chest. "Nobody here is sneezing, so no apparent allergies or problems with leaving Ribbons here for a bit."

"Just keep her on her leash. She could be a runner," Brant warned, backing through the door. "And thank you. Seriously."

"Go. We've got this," Karen said, warmed at the thought of getting to dog-sit for a little while.

Two kids had taken Ribbons's leash and led her toward the beanbag chairs. The dog chose a pink one, and the other children jostled for spots next to their special guest. Faith began retelling the story Karen had moments ago, doing a pretty good job of "reading" it from memory, holding the book in front of Ribbons so she could see the pictures.

Karen took the end of the abandoned leash and looped it around a table leg in case the dog was indeed a runner. As she sat back at her computer, she found herself distracted by the sounds of joy coming from the corner. The library needed a dog.

She took a photo of the kids reading to the dog and, with permission from the moms, posted it on the library's social media account, getting instant replies about how wonderful it was.

It felt all too soon when Brant returned for Ribbons.

"How'd she do?"

He and Karen stood by the circulation desk, watching the now quiet group of kids playing near the sleeping dog.

"She did great. The children read to her the whole time. You can definitely mark her down as kid-friendly."

"Great. Thank you."

Feeling as though she was prying, but unable to help herself, Karen asked, "Is Myles okay?"

"Okay?" Brant seemed surprised.

"Yeah. He just seems… different… sometimes."

"Different how?" Brant shifted from foot to foot.

Maybe Myles was just tired. They'd had some long days and nights on the heels of a long week of working hard. She needed to go slow and steady with cowboys. She'd learned that already.

"Never mind." She smiled and shook her head.

"But he's acting odd?"

She thought back to how something had shifted the night of the double date, and how things didn't quite add up so she could put her finger on what she'd done to change things. It was like he couldn't read, except she knew he could. There was something there, but she just couldn't figure it out.

"Well, it's like everything's great," she found herself saying, as Brant watched her, his expression patient and open. "Really great. But sometimes he just shuts down on me. I get that we're different, but it's like I've done something wrong. Stepped in a pothole or something. You know?"

Brant was silent for a long moment. "I think maybe you need to talk to Myles. And be persistent. He likes you."

"I was just hoping for some insights," she said quietly, hating the way she sounded so broken and lost.

"It's probably best to get insights straight from the horse's mouth. I don't want to speak out of turn."

Which meant there was something going on.

"You have cats, but no dog?" Brant asked, as Karen finally led the sleepy animal over from the beanbag chair. "You seem natural with her."

"We had dogs growing up. Anytime you want to bring her by, go ahead." She had adored having the dog here. Ribbons was quiet, cute and obedient. Better than most patrons. "She was good for the kids." She smiled. "And me, too."

Ribbons had been the highlight of her day. Even the crotchety William Fisher had stopped to pet the dog, even though Ribbons had been nervous around his wheelchair. With damp eyes, he'd explained that his own dog had had a run-in with Bill the armadillo last week, and how worried he'd been.

Somehow, in that small moment, Karen felt as though she'd finally connected with the man. In fact, the dog made her feel more connected with everyone today. She didn't want to lose this community, and she didn't want to lose Myles. She wanted to fight to keep it all, and that meant she needed to stop fretting and mooning over where things were right now with Myles, and put her attention squarely on making the fair as successful as possible so she could remain in Sweetheart Creek. The rest would sort itself out.

10

*M*yles was exhausted. The fair was tomorrow and it felt like all he'd done was take care of things on the ranch, practice football with the team and follow Karen's explicit instructions as she checked items off her never-ending to-do list.

Levi had left town again a few days ago to tag along with Laura as she worked on some deals in California. They planned to stop and visit Betty's daughter, the famous actress, Janet Keyes to see how her recovering husband was doing after a recent accident. The timing of their trip certainly hadn't made things easier where the ranch was concerned. The couple planned to return tomorrow night in time for the dance, and Myles had to admit he was a little envious of the way his brother was now stepping away from ranch work and responsibilities to enjoy himself. Myles was used to being the one who could do that, with Levi there to pick up any pieces dropped in his absence. If Myles needed to travel with the football team, or spend extra time with Ryan working out practice plans and strategies, Levi had been there.

Now Myles was the one picking up the slack, and he wasn't

sure how Levi had done it with such apparent ease and grace. Not that his brother hadn't complained about it, but he'd made it look easy.

"Ryan, I need your help on the ranch," Myles said into his phone, while stifling a yawn. He needed more coffee, but had already consumed a potful before his mother came over to the main house to make breakfast. He, Hank and Owen, the two ranch hands, had completed the chores in record time, but there was still more to do, especially since tonight's football game—an important one that could either end their season or send them on to bi-district playoffs—was being held an hour away, adding two hours of travel time to Myles's already busy day.

There was a half beat where Myles figured Ryan was either dreaming up an excuse to get out of helping, or deciding out how he could manage to swing by on a Friday morning when he had classes in a few hours.

"I'll be there in fifteen."

"You know how to fix that windmill Levi was going on about not working, right?" Myles asked, before his brother ended the call.

"The one up by Devil's Horn?"

"Yeah. It's on the fritz again and Hank's already moved the herd back into that pasture." A pasture without water. Not good.

"Okay. Wait for me in front of the house. I think I know what's wrong."

As Myles grabbed one of his mother's oatmeal squares from the fridge and found his truck keys, he wondered why Ryan hadn't just fixed the windmill weeks ago if he knew what the problem was. His brother was the best at fixing things around the ranch, but also the least interested, if you didn't count Cole and his disappearing act.

A few weeks ago Levi had told them all to decide what stake they wanted in the ranch or he'd buy them out. Myles had told him he was happy with keeping his share and helping out. Brant, too. But Ryan? Myles was pretty sure he wasn't going to give a straight answer until Levi imposed a firm deadline.

Myles checked his phone for the time. Karen had taken the day off to do last-minute things for tomorrow's fair, and he'd promised he'd be all hers after he finished chores. He just hoped that by the time she was done with him there would be enough left in his tank to make it through tonight's game, so the undertaker wouldn't be shoveling dirt over him by midnight.

Myles put toolboxes and a few of the usual items needed to service and fix windmills into the back of his truck, and went to wait for Ryan, waving to Betty as he passed the riding stable. When he parked in front of the rambling ranch house, Buckey came trotting over from where she'd been sitting on the porch with Lupe. Myles stepped out and held the door so his dog could jump in, then stood beside the truck and checked his phone, figuring there was probably stuff from Karen to deal with.

She had sent him so many documents over the past few days, lists and lists of things to do. He'd take one look at them and feel a headache coming on. In the end he'd have his phone read the documents to him, then he'd dictate his thoughts back to Karen. It was agonizingly slow, but not as bad as struggling to read them himself.

Ryan's Jeep turned down the driveway and moments later parked beside Myles's truck. "Hey, Buckey," his brother said, climbing into the passenger side of Myles's truck, patting her. Ryan had a dog Brant had found for him, but he didn't come to the ranch very often, preferring to stay home to bark at pedestrians from the front window of Ryan's small bungalow.

Myles climbed in, started the truck and put it in gear. They drove past the stables and machine shed, and out into the open grasslands beyond. Ryan hopped out as needed to open gates, letting Myles drive through before closing them again to keep the various herds in the right pastures.

"That stampede on Levi's birthday was something, huh?" Ryan

said at one point, referring to the cattle that had gotten out, then been chased by Laura's dog, Target, right through the birthday party happening on the back patio. Levi's girlfriend had been mortified, certain the whole town was laughing at her. For a while Myles had thought she wasn't ever going to show her face again, and he'd worked with Levi to remove all traces of land-scaping damage to help appease Laura's feelings of guilt. As far as he could tell, it had helped. Or maybe it was the power of their love that had overcome the humiliation of the ruined party.

"How are things going with the fair?" Ryan asked as they pulled up next to the windmill in need of repairs. "Details killing you yet?"

"I don't think Karen's slept in a week. She's our details person, and last Saturday night it was like someone set fireworks off under her. She created this big color-coded schedule for volunteers and then had it filled within a day."

She'd obviously tired of him, though. Her focus was securely locked on the fair at all times rather than stealing kisses from him. Myles felt as though she must have worked him out of her system at some point during the week. Maybe she'd seen through him and decided their differences were too great to overcome. He'd caught her expression in the library when he'd bowed out of reading to the kids, his excuse being the trailerload of tables. Tables that could have waited, as she likely knew.

He sighed. A braver man would tell her the truth, not dance around it in hopes that it would never matter to her—a woman whose entire life was predicated upon what he was dedicating significant energy into avoiding.

Why did she have to be a librarian?

"Need any help tomorrow?" Ryan asked.

"I'm sure we could use extra hands for those unplanned things that always seem to pop up."

"I'll be there at 7:00 a.m. after I finish chores with Hank, Owen and Blake. Rodeo grounds, right?"

"Yeah. Thanks."

Levi may have depended on Cole throughout the years until their fallout, but Myles counted on his little brother. If Ryan ever left the way Cole had, Myles was pretty sure he'd be close behind. He didn't want to think about the time they'd almost lost Ryan in a flash flood when he was seven. Myles, only two years older, had jumped in after him without thinking, paying no heed to the risks. That was what you did for the people you loved. You took risks. You put your life on the line when theirs was in danger.

Wordlessly, the brothers got out of the truck and began working on the windmill. Ryan focused on the task of tinkering, while Myles handed him tools, the two of them bent over the windmill's gears. They were just about done when Ryan let out a yelp.

"What are you doing?" he demanded accusingly, his brows pushed together in anger.

Myles visually checked his brother's fingers in case he'd absently allowed something to slip, pinching him in the process. "What do you mean?" he asked, as Ryan stood and whirled.

"Git!" He was shooing a goat. "Whose animal is this?"

Myles glanced toward Buckey, who didn't seem at all concerned about the five goats wandering around, one of them focused on the seat of Ryan's jeans, trying to score another nibble.

Myles leaned against the gearbox and laughed.

"It's not funny."

Oh, it was. The Billy kept reaching, its eyes huge as Ryan backed away, angling this way and that as the animal went in for another sample.

"They probably belong to the ranch next door," Myles said, lowering himself into the shade of the windmill's crank box to watch the antics. "Mom said something about a hobby rancher moving in. The name's Clarke or something like that."

"Seriously?" Ryan said, jumping to the left. "Hasn't he heard of a fence?" He called to Buckey, "Get over here and act like a ranch dog!"

Buckey looked up, then shoved her nose back down a pocket gopher's hole.

"I've heard goats are pretty good at escaping," Myles said, scratching one of the nannies behind her ears and getting a happy bleat in return.

"I don't care!" Ryan was still trying to shoo the one away from him.

"They'll probably return home on their own."

"I don't like them roaming around. They're eating grass our cattle need."

There was that. And they could cause damage. Not just to Ryan's backside.

"Where's Lupe? Shouldn't he be out here herding them back home?" Ryan asked.

"He's probably moping on the front porch, waiting for Levi to return." The Australian shepherd brooded whenever Levi left, which until lately hadn't been that often.

"I ought to go talk to that new rancher and tell him how things go here in Texas."

"He's not from Texas?"

"Can't be. Letting his goats get loose like this."

Myles kept his mouth shut, knowing full well there had been times where he and Brant had been sent over to replant a neighbor's gardens when their herds had broken a fence, or flash floods had lifted cows over fences that crossed normally tame creeks.

"The windmill's turning," he announced, looking up as a sound alerted him of motion.

Ryan cursed and lunged for the gearbox, sliding a pin into place. He, too, looked up at the turning blades. "Any water coming out?"

"Yep. Nice and clear," Myles said, walking around to where a stream was gushing from a pipe into a large trough. "Why didn't you fix this earlier?" The windmill had been causing him and Levi nothing but grief for weeks now.

Ryan shrugged. "I've been busy with stuff."

"What kind of stuff?" It was typically either women or his latest scheme on how to take over the world.

"Ideas."

By Myles's guesstimate his youngest brother should be close to paying off his student loans as well as the mortgage on his house by now. He always had various projects and schemes on the go. He'd get a look in his eye, like he was planning something in the back of his mind and wasn't fully present. Then he'd disappear for a few days, after which he'd be back, engaged and alert to what was going on around him again. Lately he'd been mentally absent, which meant he was onto something or else preoccupied with thoughts of football playoffs.

"What are you working on?"

"When was the last time the water was tested up here?" he said, changing the topic.

Myles turned his attention to the windmill again, fully aware that Ryan would share when he wanted to. Which might be never. He was on a quest, yearning for something that always seemed to be burning under the surface, though Myles wasn't sure if it was independence, wealth or none of the above. Either way, he was pretty sure he'd know when his brother achieved it.

"Levi's been keeping records in that binder in the stable office." They had to watch for harmful bacteria growing in the wells they pumped for the herds.

Myles checked the time. "I have to get to town," he added.

"Convince Karen to marry you yet?" his brother asked drily, and when Myles rolled his eyes, Ryan said, "Well, I hope this fair works out. You two have put a lot into it."

The truth was that if it didn't work, Karen would probably be moving away. And given how things had gone lately that would be the end of their relationship. Assuming they still had one. She'd been the utmost professional for the past week, and Myles missed the way she used to lean into him for a quick kiss.

"Women like gifts," Ryan said, almost to himself. "Money, too. They really like money." He glanced toward the sun, wincing at the brightness. "Although the good ones might care a bit less about that."

"Flowers?" Myles suggested, curious where his brother was going with this line of conversation.

"Yup. And jewelry."

"Or if you're Brant, a dog?"

They laughed. Their brother the vet was good at matching women with their new furry best friend.

"Who did he buy that house for?" Myles wondered aloud.

Ryan shrugged.

Last month Brant had bought Luanne Blackburn's house from Laura, sending Levi into a tailspin. Brant had let it slip that he'd bought it for someone. So far none of the brothers seemed to know who.

"So, you going to get her flowers or something?"

"Yeah, or something," he said, smiling as a plan came to mind.

He knew exactly where to find the very thing that would show Karen just how important she was to him.

ON THE DAY of the fair, Karen shivered under the rodeo grounds' floodlights and hugged her cardigan closer around her body. The sun had yet to rise and it felt as though she and Myles and their volunteers had been here completing the fair's setup only hours ago. She checked her watch. Five hours ago, to be exact. Now she was back, ready for everyone else to arrive so they could accomplish all the last-minute things before the fair opened.

A truck zoomed into the parking area, coming to a sudden

halt beside her car. Myles hopped out with a smile, looking happy and more bright-eyed than he had a right to. And how on earth did that man always make her heart patter faster, even when she was up to her eyeballs in distractions?

There was no avoiding thinking about him, and she hoped that the fair raised enough to keep her in this community for many years to come.

Myles was carrying two takeout cups of what she hoped was coffee from The Longhorn Diner. He came close and kissed her on the cheek. She savored the warmth of his skin touching hers and inhaled, leaning into the brief encounter.

He gave her a small smile, handing her one of the cups. He seemed shy, careful, no doubt having noticed how she'd tried to keep some distance between them this past week so she could focus. Today was do-or-die in so many ways it made her stomach roll.

She placed her free hand against his cheek, gratitude filling her for the man who had done so much without even being asked. She knew the toll the fair had taken on him, the dark smudges under his eyes growing each day without one complaint from him. He was so much more than she'd ever allowed herself to believe he could be.

"Thank you for your help with everything." She lowered her hand, and he licked his lips, his eyes dark with something that swung between affection and longing. "I really appreciate it."

"Of course." He tapped her cup with his in a toast. "To saving the library and having more fun than is legally acceptable today."

"What did you put in the java?" she joked, taking a sip. Nothing but wonderful life-giving, early morning coffee.

"Oh, before I forget," he said, shifting so he could dig down inside his jeans pocket. "I have something else for you." He grew silent as he looked at the object he'd retrieved.

She edged nearer to see what it was. The light from above them glinted off a band of darkened silver. Myles held it up and her heart lifted with pleasure as she realized it was a piece of jewelry.

"It had your name on it," Myles said, holding it out to her.

She accepted it, turning it in her fingers, looking for her name. The silver bracelet, slightly tarnished, was about three quarters of an inch wide and had intricate flowers and dragonflies embossed into its surface. It was beautiful, and possibly an antique.

"What do you mean, it has my name on it?"

"My grandma Ruth told me when I was in high school to give it to a woman I cared for, and who looked at me like..." He had taken the bracelet to help her slide it over her hand while they juggled their coffees. Karen waited, unsure if he was considering whether to tell her the truth or trying to remember what his grandmother had said.

"Looked at you how?" she asked quietly.

Myles took a step back as she admired the bracelet. It fit her perfectly.

He bounced on the balls of his feet ever so slightly. "It doesn't matter. It's for you."

She moved close, placing a hand on his arm. "Tell me."

"It's cheesy."

"I like cheesy."

"She just said to give it to someone who looks at me like I'm more than what everybody else sees. That's all. It was a grandma thing. Nothing weird. I don't expect it to make any sense."

Karen blinked back tears of gratitude as she stared at the bracelet. The man was nearly thirty years old, and in the long parade of wonderful, gorgeous women he'd dated, she was the first one to make him feel as though she really saw him?

She inhaled slowly, unable to speak.

"She would have liked you. We used to sit in the kitchen, and she'd bake cookies while I fumed at my homework." He was quiet for a moment, then kicked into what she thought of as cowboy mode, battening down the emotional hatches, saying dismissively, "It's just a bracelet that's been laying around. It's about time someone wore it." He took a big gulp of his coffee and winced.

Karen wasn't sure what this beautiful bracelet meant to Myles on a deeper level, but hoped she'd be able to stay living in town so she could fully explore exactly what it did. She closed the final distance between them, pulling him into her arms the best she could without spilling her coffee, then kissing him slowly.

Like his grandmother had said, she did see him differently. He was more than a cowboy, more than a jock who coached football. He was a man who saw what was important in her life, and when her courage failed, lent her everything she needed to carry on and make it happen.

She didn't want to think what her life would be like in a month or two if she hadn't met Myles, and if Jackie hadn't helped push them together.

"I should give you gifts more often," Myles said, resting his forehead against hers when they finally broke apart, his left hand warm against her lower back.

Nobody could kiss like Myles Wylder.

Snug in his arms, she realized her coffee cup had tipped, partially spilling as they'd kissed.

"So this was your grandma's?" She lifted the wrist with the bracelet.

"It was."

Again she contemplated what it meant to have accepted it, what their future might look like if today didn't go as well as they hoped. "Are you sure it's okay to give it to me?"

"Do you like it?"

"It's beautiful."

"Then it's yours."

She felt warm and nervous, happy and scared. Which pretty much described how she typically felt around Myles. Slightly out of control, like she was standing up in a convertible, no seat belt, arms stretched out in the air as the wind caressed her, buffeted her, leaving her exhilarated, slightly in danger, and having the time of her life.

———

MYLES SAT on the seat above the dunk tank and focused on the people milling about the rodeo grounds rather than on the next person in line holding a yellow ball. He had been dropped into the tank of freezing water enough times that he was close to shivering despite the unseasonably warm mid-November day. He'd filled the tank yesterday morning, hoping the water would warm up some before he got dumped into it today. Twenty-four hours clearly hadn't been enough time.

A ball whizzed past his head, far from the target that would unhinge his seat and send him sliding into the water.

From his vantage point he could see the crowd swelling, the community coming out in droves to support the library and have some fun. The food booths were lined up, the goat-petting zoo being run by the new neighbor was busy, and the rides and games all crowded as well. Even Carmichael had come out, and by the looks of it, had won a stuffed purple unicorn at the ring toss game.

Doing some quick math, Myles figured that based on entrance fees alone their costs were more than covered, meaning they were firmly into raising-money territory. And they still had the dinner and dance to go tonight.

This was going to work. No financial losses, and enough profit to keep the library doors open a bit longer, as well as keep Karen close to him.

A ball nicked his knee.

"I'm going to get you this time," Daisy-Mae called. She was spinning the last ball in her hands with a sly smile. Myles focused on her, realizing that the two missed shots had been merely to get his attention. She'd been playing softball for years, and he was pretty sure she could knock him into the water whenever she wanted to.

The question was did she want to?

"I'm happy here. Don't feel you need to hit that target, Daisy-Mae."

"*Are* you happy?"

He felt the weight of her words and nudged the brim of his straw hat, exposing his face to the heat of the sun. "I am."

"How happy?"

"Happy right where I am."

"A date with me might make you happier."

"I'm seeing someone, Daisy-Mae." Wasn't he?

"Are you exclusive?"

"You know I can only handle one woman at a time."

Daisy-Mae inhaled, her shirt rising to reveal a wider band of tanned midriff, her own straw cowboy hat shading her long curls. She seemed to be debating something.

She pulled back her arm, left foot lifting. Myles focused on the yellow ball, braced for impact with the water. The ball hit him square in the forehead.

"Hey! That hurt."

"Get your head checked," Daisy-Mae said mildly, turning away as the next person in line stepped up. It was little Faith, from the library.

"You can come closer," he said, waving to her. He didn't think the four-year-old was much of a threat, but even if she was, going into the water would be worth the feeling of pride she'd receive for hitting her target.

Faith solemnly shook her head, carefully adjusting her feet so they remained behind the yellow line spray-painted in the grass.

"It's okay," he said. "Kids can come on this side of the line to throw."

She threw the first ball, and it bounced off the ground in front of the tank.

Myles leaned forward, ready to jump in if her ball got close to the seat-releasing target. Faith quickly threw her second and third balls.

"Oh, that's too bad," he said, when they landed short of the tank. "Maybe next time."

She shook her head, brown eyes large. "I didn't want to get you more colder. I just want to help the library."

Talk about breaking his heart.

"Thank you, Faith." He nodded to her mom, who smiled and took her hand, promising her cotton candy.

He watched them go, thinking about how much this day was probably costing the family of two. Times were tough in their household, and yet here they were, supporting the library and the community. Just like the community would do for them, if need be.

A ball whizzed close to the target, sending a twang through the air. The seat rocked. Myles turned to see who was next in line.

Ryan. Great. He was going back into that icy tank for sure.

His brother asked with a wicked smile, "How's the water?"

"It's freezing. If you send me in, I'll owe you one."

Ryan smirked and threw the ball again. He narrowly missed the target.

He was toying with him.

"I'm still bigger than you are!" Myles threatened.

Ryan continued to smirk.

Karen was hustling past in adorable khakis, a white blouse, and a cowboy hat that was pulled down low. Myles whistled to her, curious about the hat. He hadn't ever seen her in a cowboy hat before. It looked hot on her, and he wondered what it meant that she was wearing one.

She kept on walking.

"Hey, good looking!" She was just about out of earshot when he called again. "Karen!"

She turned, spotting him quickly.

"Here." Ryan held out his handful of balls to her. He'd bought extra, possibly as a way of finally getting even for that time when, aged thirteen or fourteen, he had sneaked a few beers at their grandfather's sixty-fifth birthday party and gotten tipsy. The brothers had tied their underage sibling to a lawn chair and sprayed him with the garden hose to "help sober him up" so Carmichael or their parents wouldn't tan his hide. Come to think of it, Ryan's disgusting homemade Lambic beer could be a subtle method of retribution for the same incident.

"Wait. What are you doing?" Myles asked, as Karen took the balls, swapping them for her clipboard. Behind them a few people cheered her on. She glanced at Ryan, who was still smiling, and then at Myles.

"Knock him in," Ryan commanded.

The group behind him took up the chant.

Karen angled up to the yellow line. Ryan whispered something in her ear and she smiled, before turning toward Myles with a dangerous look in her eyes.

"You wouldn't," he said, feeling cornered on his perch. "Karen. Please."

"It's important that I be seen supporting the library," she said seriously.

"Having those yellow balls means somebody paid for them. You don't have to actually throw them to show your—"

Splash!

Myles popped to the surface with a gasp. That water was not getting any warmer, that was for certain. He snagged his floating hat, sending it sailing onto dry ground while hoisting himself out as quickly as humanly possible, his breath caught in his chest. That tank was as cold as the flooding creek had been the time he'd jumped in after Ryan.

JEAN ORAM

His shirt stuck to him and his shorts dripped freezing water down his legs like a waterfall. Myles climbed down the ladder onto the grass and squeezed out his clothing, still gasping from the cold.

Karen was whooping, everyone cheering and Ryan doubled over laughing.

"Glad you enjoyed that," he muttered. "Ryan, didn't you say you wanted to help out today?"

His brother backed up so fast he nearly tripped. He touched his hat. "New hat. Sorry. Can't." He was gone in a flash.

Karen was trying not to smile, but looked immensely pleased with herself.

"I thought you said you weren't athletic."

"I'm not! I swear that was a fluke!"

Myles lunged for her, sweeping her into a giant hug. She squealed and laughed, writhing to break his hold, her bracelet warm against the back of his neck as she reached out to brace herself. He placed a kiss on her cheek, wishing he had aimed for her mouth.

Her eyes sparkled as she looked at him, and the stress of the past few days that had erected a wall between them suddenly lifted. The sun broke out from behind a cloud and a ray of heat surged through him. And just like that, everything in his world felt right once more.

KAREN WAS GETTING wet and cold, pressed against Myles's sopping body and she didn't care one bit. She gripped his hair with one hand while holding her cowboy hat on her head with the other, tugging him in for another kiss.

What was it about this man? He was tender but demanding. Strong and yet vulnerable. And today? The whole event was happening because of him. Their costs were covered and they were strictly in the black, every dollar that came in going straight to the library from here on out for the rest of the fair.

Because of Myles.

And because of him the library would be safe for another few months at least, allowing time for another miracle to sweep in and do its part. But most of all, she was going to be able to stay here in Sweetheart Creek with Myles.

She gave him another kiss, taking her time, until the people who had lined up to knock Myles into the tank began to protest.

Reluctantly, she pushed away, saying, "You'd better get back up there."

He gave the brim of her hat a playful pat. "When's your turn?" he asked, walking backward toward the ladder.

She picked up her clipboard from where Ryan had abandoned it in the grass, pretending to check her list. "I don't seem to see myself on the tank's schedule."

"We can fix that," Myles said, coming back over to her, hand poised to take the pen. "I see you're wearing a sensible white shirt, which will be popular."

She looked down quickly, gasping when she realized the front of her shirt was so wet it was practically transparent. She scowled at Myles, mortified, as she pulled the fabric away from her skin and bra.

"It's all about the fundraising, right?" he said, with a wink that made her burn.

"Miss Hartley!" Henry said sharply. She'd run into him a few times and it seemed the busier and more successful the fair got, the crankier he became. "We have an issue with the cotton candy machine." He caught sight of her shirt. "And your blouse!"

Myles stepped in front of her, blocking Henry's view of the outline of her bra as he shucked off his T-shirt, wrung it out and handed it to her.

"Thank you for letting me know," Karen said primly. She wrestled her way into Myles's shirt, trying to keep her eyes from running down his bare torso, memorizing contours and muscles she'd love to touch.

"Henry, want a turn in the tank?" Myles asked.

His great-uncle harrumphed and carried on.

"Thanks," Karen said with a shiver, gesturing to the clinging shirt.

Myles took in her appearance with a chuckle, rubbing a palm idly across his chest. If she didn't know any better, she'd say he liked the way she looked in his wet shirt.

"Don't get used to seeing me in this," she said, cheeks burning.

"No?"

"Uh-uh. I'm going to head over to Jenny's booth now and buy a new shirt." She paused for effect. "And for future reference, I prefer my boyfriend's shirts to be dry." She turned on her heel, pleased with her retort, and just about bumped into a line of women ogling Myles and waving their money at the kid in charge of dunk tank tickets.

"That can be arranged," Myles called after her. "I have a full wardrobe. Come on over anytime, night or day, and take your pick. Although, come to think of it, you're also welcome to whatever I happen to be wearing."

11

*M*yles had been so busy at the dinner, then at the dance, greeting people, answering questions and ensuring things were moving as they were supposed to, that he'd barely seen Karen. The caterer had taken away the dessert plates, cleared the dance floor of tables, then put out snacks as the band started playing. Myles had checked on the bartenders, the team working the door, the band, the MC, and even the people working the silent auction and raffle tables. Karen had given everyone such thorough instructions there were no longer any questions for him to field, making him think it was time to let loose and enjoy a few dances with Karen like his mom had suggested.

Unable to find Karen, he took Daisy-Mae, his mother, then Jackie out for a turn around the floor, doing his best to avoid the gaggle of women who called to him whenever he strode by, begging him to take a break and dance with them, too. He noted that Garfield Goodwin, Mrs. Fisher's most reliable tipper, had taken her out for a spin. She'd looked uncomfortable at first, but had been smiling by the end of the song, just as his mother had been after her dance with Clint.

Finally, Karen went whizzing past, her beautiful blue, sleeveless dress flowing around her legs. The way the skirt was cut made him think of salsa dancing, and he admired the teasing glimpses of her exposed flesh as she moved.

He took a couple quick steps to catch up with her, then snagged her hand. "Have I told you how gorgeous you look in that dress?" he whispered in her ear.

"You're still thinking about that?"

So he'd told her a few times already.

"Want to dance to see if it helps distract me?"

"I have to run this to the band." She waved an envelope. He was fairly certain it was the remainder due after the deposit for playing tonight.

"They're in the middle of a set."

"There are a lot of things to do," she said, slipping her hand from his with a warning look.

"What can I do to help?"

"Take a breather. I'll find you when I need you."

Myles leaned against a wall near the bar and tapped his foot to the beat. He wanted to dance. With Karen. Nobody else.

He watched her mount the steps at the side of the stage, slip around the curtain and disappear. The MC, local DJ Davis Davies, was sitting on the steps, enjoying a beer and chatting with Carmichael, who, based on his expression, didn't appear to be able to hear a thing the man was saying.

Karen reappeared, spoke with Davis, then worked her way back to Myles. "We're going to do a quick thing onstage in about fifteen minutes. Don't go anywhere." She flashed him a quick smile, her gaze trailing down his outfit. He'd chosen a black Western-style shirt, new jeans, cowboy boots and his black hat. Honestly, he'd expected a bit more reaction to his outfit.

Granted, she was busy. And it wasn't always all about him.

But he wanted it to be where she was concerned.

She hustled off again and a moment later Levi leaned against the wall beside him. His brother and Laura had arrived home that day, and Myles was fairly certain she had made a hefty contribution, as their donation jar, at last count, held about two thousand dollars more than even the best barn dance of the season.

"You tell her yet?" Levi asked.

"Tell who what?"

"Karen." He tipped his chin toward her. She was smiling, holding up a book written by a local author and posing alongside Polly Morgan for a newspaper photo.

Myles gave a small shake of his head. That "something" he hadn't told her was the reason he knew he'd never quite be the man Karen hoped to fall in love with.

"She's nice," Levi said.

"She is."

"Mom really likes her."

The reporter moved on and Alexa, Nick, Laura and Maria joined Karen and Polly. Karen looked like part of the family. Happy and comfortable.

Their mom gave Karen a hug, then caught her wrist as the hug ended. Myles saw the recognition in Maria's eyes as she gazed upon her late mother-in-law's bracelet. She didn't appear to react other than to admire it, getting a shy smile from Karen. Then his mother scanned the room, no doubt on the lookout for him. He shifted to face Levi, turning his back to her.

"You know she'll still like you whether you tell her or she figures it out," Levi said gently. "It's just a matter of which way you want it to go."

"I want her to more than like me." That was the problem. He'd seen the way she'd reacted in the bookstore when he'd tried to tell her he wasn't ever going to be the bookworm she was. And he'd heard her loud and clear when she'd said she planned on falling for a bookworm. He'd tried audiobooks as a compromise, but they just couldn't hold his attention.

Why couldn't he have this? All of it.

Or maybe he did have this, and she already loved him just the way he was—flaws and all? He'd given her the bracelet and she'd accepted it, seeming to understand how much the gesture meant even though he'd backed out of what he was saying partway through.

"You gave Karen Grandma's bracelet?" Brant asked, coming up behind him.

Myles inhaled sharply.

"Sorry, didn't mean to startle you," he added. "So you're serious about her?"

Myles nodded.

His brother smiled. "Good. Did I tell y'all she wants to adopt Ribbons?"

And there it was. Karen might be out of Myles's league, but his brother believed in him and had accepted her like family. Otherwise, he wouldn't have given her a dog.

"Thanks, man, that means a lot." He gave him a handshake and half hug.

Ryan joined them, a drink in hand. He seemed distracted, but not the I'm-hatching-world-domination-plans kind.

"What's up?" Myles asked.

"Who's the new hottie?" He jerked his chin toward a woman chatting with the mayor and his wife. Tall and strong, with black hair and beautiful dark skin, she looked capable and held herself in a way that said she called the shots. In other words, definitely Ryan's type. "Anyone call dibs yet?"

Levi gave Ryan a dry look, which Myles echoed.

"What?" Ryan said. "Brant might have."

Brant frowned. "I don't call dibs. I'm not a caveman."

"Yeah, well. I am."

"Ever going to outgrow short-term romances?" Levi asked.

Ryan scoffed. "Like marriage is better?"

"Afraid of a little love?" Levi pressed.

"Love is overrated."

The trio of brothers gave Ryan a questioning look and he waved his glass, saying, "You fall in love. Get married on the fly. Then this life fact happens—women leave. They take off with everything that's not nailed down. What man has time in his life plans to deal with that crap?"

"What?" Myles asked. There was something in Ryan's tone that made him think he was speaking from experience. Except his brother had never been married.

"You know, Mom and Dad are happier now," Brant pointed out.

Ryan gave him a blank look.

"Dad and Sophia. Mom and Clint. It's weird, right?" Myles patted Ryan's shoulder. "And it sucks that our parents split, but that's the way it goes sometimes."

"What?" Levi whirled toward him, brows drawn together. "Clint's a thing? For sure?"

Myles shrugged, uncertain how involved they were. "They're friends."

"Friends who flirt a lot," Brant added, with a smile that made Levi's frown deepen.

"She's cute, though," Myles said, pointing to the woman Ryan had been eyeing earlier. "Beautiful, actually."

"Go talk to her," Brant suggested, nudging Ryan.

The woman waved at someone, a wedding band flashing.

"Oops. Too late on that one, Ryan," Levi said with a smirk. "Looks like she believes in love, marriage, commitment, teamwork and all that stuff you run away from."

"Seriously." Ryan shook his head. "Is everyone around here married?"

"We're getting to that age," Brant murmured.

"There's always Jackie. She's still single," Levi said, taking a sip of his drink to mask his smile.

Ryan threw him a dark look. "Why do I hang out with you halfwits?"

As the song that was playing ended and the band announced the end of their set, Karen appeared at Myles's elbow and pulled him toward the stage. "Sorry, guys, I need your brother."

"Take him," Levi said.

"Don't bring him back," Brant called out.

"Keep him!" Ryan hollered.

Subtle. Real subtle.

"You look beautiful tonight," Myles said to Karen. "Have I told you that already?"

"Several times, as I'm sure you told all those women you danced with." She was focused, nervous. Not that warm, passionate gal who'd been kissing him in the cold, dark parking lot before dawn.

"You deserve to be told that all day long. And you're right. My mom does look beautiful tonight and I told her as much on our second dance." He tugged Karen's hand to see if she would turn, allowing him to pull her into his arms.

Nope. She was heading toward the stairs, a woman on a mission.

Davis handed Karen his microphone at the center of the stage, and Myles joined her under a spotlight. The bowl of tickets for the draw was ready and waiting for them.

"Thank you, everyone, for coming. And a big thank you to our volunteers and donors," Karen said. She looked uncomfortable, her smile slightly forced.

"The band will be playing one more set," Myles announced, when she blinked out into the crowd, seeming to have forgotten what they'd come onstage to say. "While they take a break we'd like to do a draw."

"We have some lovely door prizes contributed by local businesses as a thank you for your support."

"And because prizes are fun!" Myles said, leaning into the microphone. In reply, he received a joyful hoot from someone in the audience.

"Jenny Oliver from Blue Tumbleweed has donated a pair of cowboy boots of the winner's choosing," Karen said quickly.

"And that winner is…" Myles said, placing his hand in the fishbowl of raffle tickets and making a show of mixing the bits of paper. He pulled one out and handed it to Karen to read into the microphone. Someone in the back let out a whoop.

"Who's our winner?" Myles asked.

A hand waved above the turning heads, and a tall woman appeared as the crowd parted for her to come forward.

"Laura Oakes!" Myles declared. "I've heard you could use a proper pair. Oh, wait. My brother Levi already bought you some." He turned to Karen, pretending he wasn't still talking into the microphone, but just to her. "Maybe we should swap this gift certificate for the one from the jewelry store in Riverbend? I think these two need an engagement ring more than another pair of boots."

Karen shook her head in alarm, and the audience laughed.

There was no gift certificate from the jewelry store.

"Well, either way, I think the next thing Levi should be getting Laura should be a little smaller and much sparklier." He dangled his left hand in the air and wiggled his bare ring finger. The crowd roared with laughter on cue, and Karen tipped her head to the side, looking exasperated yet amused.

"You can collect your gift certificate from Karen," Myles said, as Laura approached the stage with a smile and a good-natured shake of her head. He had a feeling that even though he teased, it truly wouldn't be long before she'd be wearing a ring from Levi.

They continued on, Karen relaxing as Myles did more and more of the speaking, drawing the final prizes including a signed hockey stick from his NHL friend Maverick Blades. As Myles drew the winning ticket for the last prize, Karen took the microphone.

"Because this is a library fundraiser," she said, the spotlight making her bare arms glow, "and because Myles and I are such supporters of literacy, as are so many of you tonight, I thought we could do a little reading."

Myles felt his core go cold. What was she talking about? This was not on any of her carefully done up lists, never mentioned in any of the plans. And a terrible idea, not only because the audience didn't want to hear literature when they'd come to party, but because it was the one thing he could not do.

———

KAREN COULD PRACTICALLY FEEL her heart pounding all the way from her fingers to her toes, the blood whooshing through arteries and veins as she stood in the spotlight, looking out at the community. Her community.

The town had been so supportive. There had been no teasing, no scoffing. Nothing but unbridled support. Even from cowboys who had confessed they'd never stepped inside her library. It felt as though she should do something from the heart, even if taking over the stage in this way filled her with terror.

But seeing as this whole day was about saving the library and about literature, it felt only right to share a piece of the arts as well as her gratitude.

"I know many of you are probably familiar with the Robert Frost poem 'The Road Not Taken,' and I thought tonight would be a good night to read it. It talks about making changes, taking risks and traveling down paths you might not normally choose. I feel it's fitting because when I first spoke about raising money to help support the library to keep its doors open, I was thinking small and safe."

She went to give Myles's arm a squeeze, but he'd edged out of reach, no longer sharing the spotlight. "Myles encouraged me to think larger, bigger."

Frustrated, she marched over, grabbed his arm and pulled him closer, so he was standing beside her. She was grateful she'd met him, that he'd stepped up to help her, as well as allowed her to peek into his soul and see the real side of himself he kept hidden away. She wanted to share that version of Myles with everyone here tonight.

"Myles Wylder is the reason we've had today's fair and tonight's dinner and dance," she said. "It also couldn't have happened without so many volunteers and the support of our community. I am so grateful for all Myles has taught me these past two weeks as we've taken the road less traveled together. And with a grateful heart and an adventurous spirit I'd like to read this poem with him."

Karen lowered the microphone and held up her phone, where the poem was displayed. She said to Myles, "I was thinking I would read a line, then you would. Or we could go stanza by stanza."

He stared at her, jaw tight. "I can't."

His quiet, flat tone sent a shiver through her.

She gave him a puzzled look, trying to sort out what was happening. He'd just wrapped the entire crowd around his finger as she'd stood there, a nervous wreck. He'd written her a poem and frequented a diner because it featured poetry. So how could he even begin to think he couldn't do this? The Myles Wylder she was falling for didn't seem to know the meaning of "I can't."

The audience was waiting, shifting, the murmurs growing louder like a swarm of approaching bees.

Karen lifted her hands in question. Was Myles flat out refusing? She'd just put it out there, everyone was waiting, and he was going to let her down? Now? After weeks of hard work? After a grueling day yesterday, when he'd worked on the ranch, then the fundraiser, then traveled to an away game, then returned to town to help her again? It made no sense.

She began reading, her voice shaking with uncertainty. She reached the end of the first stanza and tipped the phone and microphone toward Myles, hoping he'd jump in. He gently guided the phone back to her while saying into the microphone, "I think y'all would prefer if the poem was read with Karen's lovely voice, wouldn't you?"

Someone shouted something from the back of the room that brought a few laughs, and Myles's jaw tightened.

"I want to share this with you," Karen whispered. She owed him so much, and he deserved to share the spotlight, this moment.

"Y'all know cowboys don't read poetry, don'tcha?" he said slowly, his Texan accent accentuated, gaining more laughter from the crowd.

Karen's cheeks burned and she snatched the microphone and phone to her chest, turning her shoulder to him. "Fine then. It's a good thing librarians do."

Her tone was slightly snooty, and she got a few laughs as she played up her old, tired librarian role. In her periphery she could see Myles shutting down, backing away, arms extended as if to showcase her as she lifted the microphone to her lips once again.

With a trembling voice she fumbled her way through the rest of the poem, knowing she'd botched it, but feeling worse about how Myles had uncharacteristically abandoned her in the most embarrassing way. She stumbled over her words as she thanked everyone, then she fled the stage.

Cowboys don't read poetry?

Was he embarrassed to be the man she saw? The man who wasn't afraid to express his thoughts and feelings through the written word?

She gave herself a shake. It didn't matter, because he wasn't willing to be his true self, the one he was around her. When it came down to what others thought of him, she didn't matter enough that he would slough off his stereotypical cowboy image. He'd rather make her look foolish in front of everyone.

And why was that?

Because cowboys don't read poetry.

As the band came back onstage and took their places again, she hurried toward the safety of the side exit, wishing she'd never given that one special cowboy a chance to win her heart. Never given him a chance to break it.

WHAT WAS he going to do?

Myles paced outside the community center's side exit, unable to outpace the rush of humiliation pressing down on him. Did everyone except Karen know why he'd bailed out of reading her poem? Why hadn't he told her he was dyslexic? Her look of hurt and rejection had been too much.

But the shame and public humiliation of being asked to read a poem onstage with the woman he loved, and being unable to do it, was too much. He couldn't share in her joy, couldn't live up to her standards and be the man she needed.

It had been foolish to spend the last two weeks trying to be anything but who he really was.

And the poor woman had no idea, because, like the other Wylder men, he was a fabulous secret keeper. Only he and his father knew the real reason Cole had left and never come back. Levi had spent years agonizing over why, and Myles still hadn't told him, just like he hadn't told Karen the truth about himself. He knew exactly why Cole wasn't coming home again, and he knew exactly why Karen was done with him.

Myles continued to pace, shaking his head over how long he'd kidded himself. It was time to step back so Karen could find a man who could keep up with her in all the ways that mattered to her. He would help with tonight's cleanup and then just walk away.

The side door creaked open, and Myles braced himself in case it was Wade Ross coming to tell him what an idiot he was. Tonight wasn't a dry event and he had a feeling the man would be more than happy to let him know what he thought of his old tutoring client. And the worst was that it wouldn't just be Wade who thought he was foolish for trying to woo a librarian. The whole town knew he was horrible at schoolwork and reading; he'd simply done a good job of pretending that nobody remembered or cared.

Karen eased through the gap between the door and its frame, her dress almost snagging on the handle.

"What?" he snapped.

"What was that in there?" She folded her arms against the chill of the night, her dark hair silvery where the light above cast its rays. "Cowboys don't read poems? Are you embarrassed to enjoy books and to talk about literature and write poems for me? Are you so intent on being the stereotypical cowboy that you take pride in hiding your intelligence? I don't understand that mentality. I really don't. Being smart is cool, in case you didn't notice, and I thought you were more than the image you hide behind. I thought you couldn't care less about fitting in. I was wrong."

She grasped the bracelet he had given her, tugged it over her hand and pushed it against his chest. He refused to take it and it fell to the ground as she turned away, heading back inside.

Myles slowly bent to retrieve the antique piece, then scrubbed his thumb over the scratch that had formed from where it had landed on the concrete. He didn't try to go after Karen. It was too late. It wouldn't matter.

He walked along the edge of the building, heading toward where he'd parked his truck, gritting his jaw against the pain in his chest. He clung to the bracelet, willing himself to put one foot in front of the other until he reached his vehicle.

Daisy-Mae spotted him as he crossed the street.

"Myles!"

"Not now."

"You okay?"

"No."

She fell back, the sound of her heels slowing on the pavement. Then she sped up, leaping into the passenger seat when he unlocked the truck.

"If I can do anything—"

"You can't." Not this time.

He started the engine and drove off without looking back, knowing that someone would be there to help Karen with the event's homestretch.

There always was, but it wouldn't be him. It was never going to be him when it came to Karen.

KAREN STEPPED through the side exit again, unable to face the hall full of people with her eyes so damp. Myles was marching away, his strides determined as he disappeared around the corner of the building. Inside, the band was playing a slow song. Four more tunes and the night would be done. Based on her count they had raised enough to keep the library doors open for at least six months, maybe longer.

She should be happy.

She touched the bare spot on her left wrist where the silver bracelet had spent the day. This morning felt like a lifetime ago.

She'd gone from thinking Myles was the real deal to being humiliated and abandoned in front of the community.

She'd thought he cared more about her than what the towns-people thought of him. She had been so wrong. He'd allowed her to put herself out there to get laughed at, just like the jock she'd always known he was.

She would never be wrong again. She would listen to thought and reason, not her heart and emotions. And she'd have no part of steamy kisses.

"Good." She nodded emphatically and turned toward the

door, reaching for the metal handle. Her chest squeezed as a wash of emotion rushed through her. She said louder, "Good."

She tried for more firmness in her voice as she wrestled with the hurt she felt. "It's for the best. And so much better now rather than later." The sternness in her tone didn't help convince her heart that it shouldn't hurt, and that she wasn't somehow missing out on something wonderful.

The door swung open and a head peeked out. "There you are!" Jackie said brightly. She caught Karen's expression, and said, "Oh no. Did someone run off with the cash box?"

Karen shook her head.

"You didn't break even?" Jackie was watching her carefully, and Karen knew she understood exactly why she was out here moping, with tear-filled eyes that threatened to spill over.

Karen shook her head again, the tears impossible to fight. She tipped her head back and sniffed, willing that damned salty liquid back inside her eyelids.

"You almost hit Bill the armadillo and your suitcase went flying into the ditch and teenagers went rifling through your underpants? Wait, that was Laura." Jackie smiled and pulled her into a giant hug, resting her head against Karen's as she slowly rocked her, while the tears came.

"Men suck, I know," Jackie said soothingly. "Myles has problems you'll never understand."

"You can have him."

"I don't care if you just freed up a Wylder for me. If he treats you like this and makes you cry, then he's no good for anyone." Jackie held Karen in front of her. "Shall I push him in the creek next time it floods? I can make it look like an accident."

Karen hiccuped as she tried to laugh. She waved a hand in front of her eyes and nose, stepping away from Jackie. "I—I'd never ask you to put your freedom at risk by—by doing something illegal," she stammered.

"You're such a rule follower. And technically, you wouldn't

even have to ask." Jackie gave her a little grin. "Just wink twice and I'll take care of things."

Karen couldn't help but laugh. "You're the best friend ever." She gave her another hug. "Did you find anyone worthy tonight?"

"There were some good dancers out there, but nobody I plan to take home."

"Anyone you plan to see again?"

Jackie scratched her nose, looking uncharacteristically heartbroken.

"What's wrong?"

She shook her head. "Nothing."

"Who are you waiting for?"

Jackie gave her a quiet smile that seemed as sad as Karen felt.

Karen dabbed at her eyes. "Do I look like a raccoon?"

"Your makeup is fine."

She put an arm around Jackie's waist and they started walking down the narrow sidewalk that led around toward the front doors. A little more fresh air before she had to face the world again would be good. At least she hadn't cried long enough to get puffy eyes.

"You know what the problem is?" Jackie said.

"Men suck?"

"I haven't taken you to a football game. Not in an honest-to-goodness way."

Karen laughed. "Because I'm always down on the field managing the cheerleaders, you'll never get a chance."

"Then you shall die a spinster," Jackie said with a joyous giggle as they rounded the building. "You already have the cats. And I hear you and the library might get a dog."

"Pets aren't allowed in the library," Henry said sharply.

Both friends jumped, not having noticed him sitting on the bench in front, obviously looking for his own version of trouble.

Karen said, "I checked the bylaws and there's no mention of animals."

"I doubt that's true," Henry replied, straightening his back as though he planned to stand up and start throwing punches.

"Why don't we talk about it at the next meeting? Today was a very good day for the library."

"There might not be a next meeting. Other than to dissolve the whole entire organization."

"Henry," Jackie said gently, "Karen raised enough money today to save the library. If this girl wants to bring a dog to work, I think you should accommodate that. Because she *will* be working at the library. For at least another six months, from what I've heard."

Jackie turned and gave Karen a quick hug. "Congratulations on today." She waltzed inside the community center, and Karen wished she possessed the confidence Jackie demonstrated. Her friend was going to give some man a run for his money, that was for sure.

"Do you need a ride home?" Karen asked Henry.

His eyebrows lowered as he frowned. "I have a car. I'm not so old I can't drive any longer."

"Okay, just checking." Being kind to the grumpy man made her teeth hurt, but it would be too easy to get into a heated broil with him, which would do her no favors long-term.

"I saw Myles leave with that tall hussy."

Karen inhaled slowly, past the hurt, past the frustration and humiliation. She turned on her heel. "Daisy-Mae is not a hussy. She did a lot to help us today."

"I call them as I see them."

"I'm not sure that's a game you want to play," Karen warned.

"And I'm not sure what you had in mind, humiliating Myles up there with your hoity-toity literature business. But you've got another thing coming if you think you can treat my great-nephew like that!" He had stood up, his voice growing louder. His face was a dangerous red and Karen backed up a step.

"He's the one who did the hurting," she said, hating herself for taking Henry's bait. "He left me up there!"

"Henry, that's enough," Maria said sharply, marching through the doorway. She directed Karen inside, while giving her a look that seemed to be lacking its earlier warmth. Instead it was filled with concern and disappointment, making Karen think that according to the Wylder clan it hadn't been Myles who had been in the wrong, but her.

***

"I'M glad you're done playing with someone different," Daisy-Mae purred, as Myles pulled into the driveway at Sweet Meadows Ranch. The lights were off in both the main house and Carmichael's.

"What?" Myles realized he'd been tuning out Daisy-Mae for the entire drive, and without thinking, had brought her home.

"You weren't you anymore. First you were all dressed up at that barn dance. That's where it started. I missed seeing the real you."

Myles thought about who the real him might be to Daisy-Mae. A man who avoided reading. Who hid behind everyone's stereotypes because it was easier that way. A man with a future that didn't look much bigger or brighter than it had the day he'd stepped out of a high school classroom for the last time.

"I get it, though," Daisy-Mae said. "She's smart and cute and has that slightly wicked side to her. But what she did tonight was really mean."

"She didn't know."

There had been plenty of opportunities for him to spill the beans and he hadn't. He hadn't trusted Karen with the truth.

Daisy-Mae laughed. "How could she not know?"

"I hid it from her."

"She's a librarian. A book nerd." There was a twist of disbelief as well as envy in her tone.

"You ever met a Wylder who didn't have some big secret he was able to keep? Cole? Levi? Even me?"

Daisy-Mae sighed and looked out the windshield at the darkened ranch house. "Everyone knows your secret."

"Karen didn't."

"Why are you defending her? She humiliated you, Myles."

"I had it coming."

"Fine, let's not talk." Daisy-Mae gave him a sly smile and shifted from the passenger seat into his lap.

As he looked at the woman he'd sometimes turned to for distraction when reality tamped him back into his small-town box, he realized that as much as he didn't want to think about Karen, he really didn't want to kiss Daisy-Mae.

"*R*obyn! Smile!" Karen called out to the team's head cheerleader. The boys had just won their bi-district playoffs game, sending them to area playoffs. They still had four games to win to become State champions—four games in a row —but they were having a great season, something that should be reflected in the attitude of all the cheerleaders.

Technically, Karen wasn't a coach, but Rhonda didn't mind her stepping in to offer another perspective, or helpful tips. Such as smiling. Which was an odd reminder for someone like Robyn, who lived for the sport. But she was acting like Karen felt. Lifeless. Heavy. Unable to handle things she normally loved doing.

For Robyn, a hormone-ridden teenager, it was natural to have days where everything felt difficult. But for Karen to allow her whirlwind affair with Myles to impact her life was just plain silly. He'd been wrong for her all along, and yet she'd gotten caught up in his attention and the way he looked at her, and had allowed herself to believe he was the man for her and that their differences didn't matter.

And right now he was heading to the locker room with the team, yelling at his players, which was not his style. Thankfully, the cheerleaders and athletes didn't ride on the same bus, so Karen was not only saved from seeing Myles after almost a week of them not talking to each other, but also wouldn't have to be subjected to overhearing his uncharacteristic rants. He'd been quiet during the game, sitting with his shoulders hunched, hands between his knees, shaking his head. It was odd seeing him like that and she had longed to leave the cheer area and massage the knots from his shoulders. Except for the fact that he had abandoned her onstage last weekend, lied about who he was willing to be for her. And worse, she'd believed it.

As Karen waited by the cheerleaders' bus she caught sight of quarterback Blake Hernandez heading her way, hand linked with Robyn's. They had their heads bent together and were deep in conversation.

"I saw your proposal for taking in that homeless dog as if it could ever belong in the library," Henry Wylder said, coming up beside Karen.

"You follow football? Good game, wasn't it?" she said, looking around for a distraction. He had a way of getting under her skin, and during their encounter after the dance last weekend he'd managed to plant a haunting fear that she'd somehow wounded Myles onstage.

"Just because you saved the library doesn't mean it's appropriate for the library to foot the bills for your new pet. A bylaw loophole is no excuse."

"I didn't insinuate that the library should pay for Ribbons's upkeep."

She knew the library doors were remaining open, and that they were going to operate in conservation mode to stretch the new funds as far as possible.

"The board wants you to run this fundraiser again next year."

"If I do, I'll have to get paid for my time."

The man snorted and took a second look at her before snorting again and heading to his truck.

"Lovely talking to you!" she called after him, as Robyn and Blake kissed a slow goodbye. Karen remembered feeling that way, being kissed by Myles like that. She wrapped her arms around her midriff after zipping up her jacket. The November night was blustery, with rain in the forecast.

Robyn climbed aboard the cheer bus and Karen asked Blake, "How did your test go?"

"My grades are coming back up."

"Great." She'd been tutoring him a short time, and so far his biggest problem seemed to be concentration, not his ability to learn or his intelligence.

He looked shy for a moment. "I was hoping you could talk to Coach for me."

"About what?" she asked, drawing him aside so there wouldn't be eavesdroppers or interruptions. There were diehard Sweetheart Creek fans milling about. They formed convoys to each out-of-town game, and now that the season was reaching its peak even more hometown spectators were making the trips.

"Field time." Hernandez appeared remorseful.

Karen drew herself up, unsure what to say. The amount of time he got to play was not her call, and definitely not her business.

"Everything kinda got in my head lately," he explained.

"With your grades?"

"I don't know if you've heard?" He was looking at her like a small child admitting to breaking something important.

Instinctively, she shifted closer, turning her shoulder to block out anyone who might think about approaching. "About what?"

He'd had a rough season so far, and she knew the poor kid was getting it on all sides for his performance on the field, even though the team was racing toward what could be a top finish in the state of Texas.

"Robyn's pregnant," he said, just above a whisper.

Karen felt the news hit her hard in the chest. She didn't know what to say. Congratulations didn't sound right when the two seniors had life plans and possible scholarship leads. Adding a child would definitely complicate things. But a child was a gift, even if unexpected and poorly timed.

"How are you holding up?" she asked, giving his elbow a squeeze. Now she understood why Robyn had often looked unwell during their early morning practices. Why was she still on the squad? Their cheer style was more about dancing than tumbling or performing aerial tricks, but still. And the fact that Robyn hadn't felt she could confide in her... That hurt.

"She told her parents last night." The pain on Blake's face was obvious. "They're pretty upset." The youth was struggling with emotion, and Karen's heart broke for him.

"How about you and your parents?"

"They were hoping I'd make something of myself." He closed his left eye to peer at her out of his right. "But they didn't seem super surprised."

"Are you still going to try for scholarships?"

He nodded. "Coach Myles told me to keep as many options open as I could."

"Sounds smart."

"But I don't know how I'll afford it all. How will I have time to play football, go to school *and* raise a kid?"

"What are Robyn's plans?"

"She's pretty shook up still. But I love her. I'll do whatever I need to so we can make this work. And right now I need those scholarships so we have a fighting chance. I know we'll be poor and it'll be busy, but I want more for this kid. For Robyn."

Karen's heart swelled with gratitude for his determination and love. Robyn was lucky, as was he.

"What if doing the right thing means giving up football?" she asked softly.

He nodded and swallowed. "I'd do it."

Wow.

"Well, let's stick with this sport and see how far it takes you, okay? There are only a few games left."

He nodded, his shoulders relaxing.

"What did you want me to talk to Coach Ryan about? You said field time?"

She dreaded talking to Ryan and nosing in where she didn't belong, but this kid needed someone rooting for him. And if he still planned to go to college, he needed any college recruiters to see him out on the field, not sitting on the sidelines.

"Coach Myles," Blake corrected. "I talked to Coach Ryan and nothing changed. I know Coach Myles has been telling him to play other guys instead of me. Those guys need experience, too, I know, and my mind hasn't been in the game, but I'm determined now. This has got to be my focus. Saving money, studying hard, playing well and getting scholarships. I gotta do this for my family."

His determination and love were so much like Myles's it made Karen's eyes tear up. He was going to be an amazing father, an amazing partner.

"Why don't you talk to Coach Myles yourself?" she asked.

"He's quit."

"What do you mean?" He'd been there on the field short minutes ago.

"He just…" Blake shrugged. "He's usually into the game, keen to build us up so we play our best. But now it's like he's given up. Like he thinks we're a bunch of losers. Almost as if he's mad at us."

"You're not losers."

"I know. We're going to win State."

Karen smiled. Blake was watching her with an expectant expression. She softened her tone, hoping it would also soften the truth she had to deliver. "I don't think I'm the right person to speak for you when it comes to Coach Myles."

"But he likes you. He listens to you."

"We're not really talking to each other right now."

"Because of the library thing?"

The air seemed to grow still around her. She knew people were gossiping about her and Myles. She'd walked into the diner and swore half the conversations had instantly hushed, eyes darting toward her and away. Same thing in the staff room at both schools.

"Which library thing?" she asked casually, toying with her jacket zipper, hoping he'd give her a feel for what the kids were hearing about her right now.

"I heard about the fundraiser dance."

"Oh?" Nobody had breathed a word to her about the dance all week. They'd mentioned everything from the games at the fair to the dinner menu, but never the dance.

"He can't read, you know." Blake was watching her as though he was waiting for an explanation. She had a fleeting fear that his opinion of her might drastically change based on her response.

"But he can." She had seen him read.

"Yeah, but not well. He's dyslexic or something."

"No, he's not," she said automatically, even as her stomach dropped and she looked toward the players' bus in horror.

But it added up. It was that piece that had been dodging her. That would explain why he hadn't wanted all those books, why he'd asked if it mattered if he wasn't a bookworm, why he wouldn't read a poem with her onstage in front of his entire community.

Karen wanted to die when she thought how he must have felt at the fundraiser when she'd all but outed him and shone a light on his issue.

And that was why he'd looked so vulnerable and hurt when they'd talked about jocks and how cruel they could be to others. He'd felt it, faced it.

He knew what that laughter felt like, and she'd just set him up for more.

"He told me once, because I was having trouble with school-work in my junior year. He told me to get tested for dyslexia."

Karen nodded numbly, awash with guilt. Why hadn't Myles told her? Why had he felt the need to hide that from her?

"Turned out I just had an eye focusing thing and needed some exercises. I'm okay now."

"I wish I'd known that sooner," she mumbled. "About Myles."

"It's okay, Miss Hartley. We all mess up sometimes and cowboys are really good at hiding things like that." Blake smiled, and then his bottom lip quivered slightly. "But it all turns out okay in the end, right?"

Karen longed to give the boy a big, reassuring hug, but said simply, "Yes, Blake. It always turns out the way it's supposed to."

Though sometimes the way it was supposed to made your heart hurt.

ALL WEEK KAREN had been dreading the wrap-up thank-you party for the fair's volunteers out at Sweet Meadows Ranch. There was a lot to celebrate, the fundraiser having brought in enough to keep the doors open for another ten months, give the building a minor facelift as well as hold on to all current employees. She'd suggested they should skimp on shifts and skip the renovations, but the board hadn't listened. They were instead excitedly planning next year's fair and dance—two months earlier than this year's had been—as well as applying for grants that might help fill the gap they still had in their annual funding requirements.

Which meant Karen would have to go through all this all over again, except without Myles and the enormous list of favors he'd called in.

Myles. She felt a wash of shame for how she'd treated him. Talk about the worst thing she could've done to the man. She had almost called Laura and Polly and told them she was sick and unable to make it out to the ranch tonight so she wouldn't risk facing him.

Instead, she'd asked her brother to join her as a buffer in case Myles was angry. Her brother, after hearing her story, had refused to offer protection. He'd given her an encouraging pep talk and told her he'd disown her if she chickened out of going to the party to thank the volunteers whose hours of unpaid work had helped save her job.

When he'd put it that way...

So she'd gone to the city, bought a dress that was out of character, pasted on a smile she hoped didn't look too much like DC Comics' The Joker, and practiced several different ways to thank the volunteers so she wouldn't sound robotic, saying the same thing over and over again.

She was going to need these volunteers again in a few short months, and even more so since Myles was undoubtedly out of the picture.

Karen's heart ached as she parked her car in the dry grass along the driveway at the Sweet Meadows Ranch. There were lots of vehicles parked out front, couples walking across the grass to the backyard. Maybe she could have asked Glenn, an old boyfriend to come along with her. He'd been nice.

But there'd been no spark.

She reprimanded herself. There was more to life and relationships than a spark that could get out of control. Sometimes it was about finding a nice man who made you laugh and feel cared for. It would never have occurred to Glenn to keep something important from her in hopes of making her like him.

But Glenn would also never read anything as mainstream as *The Da Vinci Code.* He wouldn't allow himself to get caught up in it, as she had upon a recent rereading. She'd given the book another chance. Kind of like she hoped Myles would for her.

As Karen began making her way toward the ranch's backyard

patio, a tall, strong figure walked across the yard. For a moment her breath caught in her throat before she realized it was Myles's older brother Levi.

Why was she still reacting to thoughts of Myles? They'd barely been an item, and he had been nothing but a bad bargain for her heart.

She scolded herself, whacking invisible dust from her dress's flared skirt. The item was slightly bohemian, various scarves stitched together to create a fitted bodice and a bright, flowing and colorful skirt that was only mildly subdued by a cashmere gray wrap she wore draped over her shoulders.

"Welcome! I love your dress, Karen," Laura said, as Karen came around the corner of the house, still fuming at herself. Laura opened her arms to give her a quick hug.

"You're going to love the stuff we've added to the party. We have so much going on." She giggled, her eyes lit up. "Things kind of blossomed out of control, between Polly and me. But I think you're going to love it."

Laura led Karen under the lights strung over the patio, which had a large barbecue grill gleaming in the setting sun, new-looking outdoor furniture and freshly potted plants. Heaters were sporadically placed around the edges of the patio, warming the space.

"We have a cake that looks like a stack of books," Laura said and Karen nodded, having been the one to send the order into the bakery. "Some authors are coming in about half an hour, and are going to bring signed copies of their latest books for everyone to take home. We even invited a few of their readers to help celebrate."

"But the volunteers…" Karen frowned. The party was supposed to be a thank you for the people who'd helped out at the library's fundraising events, not a party for authors and their readers.

"It was actually one of the volunteer's ideas. It's kind of like what you wanted to do with bringing in some authors for the main event, but we didn't have time to coordinate it. Anyway, the volunteers all decided they wanted the party to be about reading and celebrating access to books and not about them." Laura's voice had grown quieter, her expression worried. "They wanted something bigger."

"Wow."

"Is that okay?"

"If they're okay with it," Karen said, feeling blown away, "then I am, too. This is really amazing, actually." She took in the party area, then turned to Laura. "You gals are totally amazing. I couldn't have done all of this without you. Not even a quarter of it."

"Aw," Laura said, giving her a half hug.

"You must be exhausted."

"Not yet, but I'm pretty sure Polly and I will fall over tomorrow when we stop running." She laughed and hugged Karen's arm. "And so you know, we think you're pretty amazing, too. You saved the library."

"Really, it was the way everyone pulled together." She glanced in the direction she'd last seen Myles. "And Myles."

Laura's smile tightened for a telling second.

Everyone was judging Karen. She could feel it.

"You kept it all coordinated," Laura said smoothly. "I know what it's like trying to keep things like that together, and you did great." With a smile she excused herself to go help in the kitchen.

Karen looked around the gathered group which was growing by the minute, searching for a friendly face. Since discovering that everyone but she had known about Myles's dyslexia, she was never sure how people would react to her. So far most everyone had been nicely diplomatic, their new reserve almost unnoticeable.

She spotted Myles standing near the glass doors that led into the house. He was talking with Daisy-Mae, who had her body pressed against his arm as she laughed. It looked like he was happily enjoying his old life again, Karen long forgotten.

She turned away and tried to focus on the person who had come up beside her.

A tall, thin man handed her a plastic cup of wine. "Thought you might like this."

"Oh, " Karen said, pleasantly surprised. She took a sip of the chilled wine. "Very thoughtful of you."

He adjusted his dark rimmed glasses, thicker than her own. "I saw a fellow wallflower and figured we should stick together."

"Oh," Karen repeated, taken aback.

"I meant that in a good way." He gave a weak smile, exposing a gap between his front teeth. He was awkward, but cute, his heart definitely in the right place. "Introverts unite!"

She tried to smile, knowing the man's efforts likely were maxing his courage if he was indeed introverted. "You like to read?"

He nodded. "And I heard you're responsible for saving the library here in town."

"It wasn't just me. Everyone helped." Her gaze slid without permission to where Myles was still standing. Daisy-Mae was leaning in, listening to him with a regretful expression that made Karen continue to watch them, until she spotted a band of old silver on the other woman's wrist. Her heart twisted sharply, causing her to gasp.

The man beside her said something meant to be humorous and she allowed a small laugh, blinking back tears as the truth settled in.

She was still in love with Myles Cameron Wylder.

MYLES STOOD and chatted with Daisy-Mae, his heart heavy as he caught glimpses of Karen talking with an obvious book nerd. He didn't mean it in a derogatory way, only that the guy was the epitome of what Myles would never be. He was likely brilliant, but also safe. He was, supposedly, what Karen was seeking.

But her smile wasn't genuine, her usual sparkle absent. She looked sad despite the attention from the man trying to coax her into laughter. He was failing. Poor man. At least he was sparing Myles's heart. He wasn't sure he could handle seeing her sparkle or break into warm laughter for someone else.

"Are you okay?" Daisy-Mae asked for the second time. He hadn't been able to shake her since he'd dumped her off his lap after coming home last Saturday. Right now she was watching him, brows drawn together in concern. She was beautiful, her hair swept up with tiny sparkly clips, her long-sleeved wool dress skimming her curves.

He was inattentive, uninterested. He was being a horrible date, and they both knew it.

"I'm sorry, Daisy-Mae."

She sighed, her bosom rising with the action. "There's not much we can do when our heart wants someone else."

He snapped his attention back to her in surprise. "What?"

"It's fine. I understand."

"No, it's not fine. I'm sorry." He renewed his grip on her hand. There was nothing wrong with Daisy-Mae, and they had been happy enough having casual fun off and on for several years now. Maybe he needed to focus and get serious about her. Maybe if he quit taking her for granted things could work out long-term.

"You look lovely tonight. Did you go to Big Hair Salon or did you do this yourself?" He lifted a hand from her waist, breathing easier as he gestured to her hair.

"Myles."

"Hmm?"

She shook her head.

"What?"

She blinked twice, her smile wobbly. "I really like you. A lot.

But I deserve someone who can give me his heart. We're not a couple of kids anymore."

"I like you, too." He squeezed her hand. "I've been distracted, I know that. You and I are alike. We're…"

"We're not alike." She seemed amused.

"We are," he insisted.

"No, we both like a good time. That's all. You've always been out of my league, you know that?"

"Me?" Daisy-Mae was the sexiest woman in the county. He was not out of her league. It was likely the other way around.

"You're smart, Myles." She pressed a hand to his chest, comfortable in his space, her body warm. "You want more in your life. And me?" She gave a half shrug. "I'm happy where I am."

"So am I."

"You're not."

"I am." His voice had risen and he lowered it again. "Don't do this."

"You already have. Your heart belongs to someone else, Myles." Daisy-Mae licked her lips, moistening them as she smoothed the fabric of his shirt over his chest. "I hope she's kinder to you the second time, and that you don't keep secrets from her."

"Who?"

She tipped her head to where Karen was patiently humoring the man trying to woo her.

Myles shook his head. "No. We're nothing. She and I are different."

"You just have different styles. You're smart, Myles. And so is she."

"She's a bookworm. I'm a dyslexic."

"And you passed school. You're not incompetent. That author over there…" She paused to find someone in the crowd, then pointed at him. "He's dyslexic! He's got what you have and he's a *writer*." She gave Myles's chest a gentle push. "Maybe it's time to get over yourself and quit hiding behind this thing so you can go be you."

Myles stared at the writer. Surely he wasn't dyslexic. Surely Daisy-Mae was mistaken.

"You can't give up because you're scared you can't keep up with her reading level, Myles. I've seen her catch a football."

Myles's attention swiveled to Daisy-Mae, on the lookout for mirth. There was none.

"Y'all have different skills and passions." She tapped his chest again, her voice softening. "You and I don't." She smiled, peering at him from under her lashes in that flirtatious way of hers. "We like beer, football and making out."

Myles tilted his head back with a sigh. He really didn't want to think about kissing Daisy-Mae, and he didn't understand why she was suddenly fobbing him off after all these years.

"You need someone who's different or you get bored."

"No, I don't."

"So why do we always seem to drift apart after we've been together for a while?"

He didn't have an answer to that, at least not one he liked.

Daisy-Mae looked at Karen with something that seemed like sadness and envy. "When you two are together it's like the air gets sucked out of the universe."

"There's no air outside the—"

"You know what I mean," she said with a flash of uncharacteristic anger. "You need someone who challenges you. And that's not me." She rolled up onto her toes and gave him a sweet kiss he knew would be their last.

"Don't do this," he whispered, his hands tight on her waist. "We can make it work."

Her palms slipped down his chest as she took a step backward, giving him a sad smile of goodbye. He caught sight of something familiar on her wrist and he snagged her hand, staring at his grandmother's bracelet, his heart thundering in his ears. "Why do you have this?"

It was wrong. So wrong. It wasn't meant for her. It would never be meant for her.

She put a hand protectively over the silver band. "It was in your truck."

He was already peeling it off her wrist, saying without thinking, "It's not for you. It belongs to someone else."

As he held the antique bracelet in his hands he felt a shudder in his chest, and a wave of grief. There was only one woman.

One.

She'd seen him as nobody else did, and it wasn't just because he'd hidden parts of himself from her. It was because she noticed what nobody else dared.

*I*n the predawn light Myles began unloading lumber and tools beside the workbench he'd set up in the parking lot of the library. The board had approved a minuscule budget so he could give the building a small facelift. He hadn't spoken to Karen at last night's wind-up thank-you party, and today, since it was Sunday, the library was closed, which meant he could easily avoid her.

The party had been fine, but it hadn't been easy seeing her in that sexy dress and being hit on by a man more her speed. Or having to face the fact that Daisy-Mae was right—he had hidden parts of himself from Karen out of fear, and as a result was as much to blame for their breakup as she was.

However, he was pretty confident she didn't want him back. She'd been clear what she was looking for, and he'd tried to fake his way into being that man. She deserved so much better than a man who was willing to lie about who he was.

He'd break his back getting the facelift done today—in time for the grand library-staying-open ceremony tomorrow—then he'd slip away and let her lead her life as she wished.

There was a lot to do, though, and he'd taken the small

stipend meant to pay him for his own time and offered it to Blake Hernandez, the dad-to-be, if he came out to help. The athlete, happy for the pay, planned to come by after church.

The plan was to fix a piece of the tin roofing, sandblast some of the building's stone front to brighten it up, freshen the paint on the window trim and entrance, as well as attach decorative shutters Myles had made for the front windows.

He'd also rebuild the broken flower boxes that butted up to the building, for the town's gardening club to plant with blooms from their own gardens. The local tree farm was donating two five-year old oak trees that would be planted south of the building to provide parking lot shade and additional greenery.

Paint and foliage would make an impressive change without costing much, and by the end of the day the library would have an inviting cottage look to it. The outside would match the welcoming feeling Karen was cultivating inside.

But Karen... He let out a sigh. He should have told her the truth, or at least replied to the invitation she'd emailed to him about tomorrow's ceremony.

He'd embarrassed her onstage, though, leaving the woman he loved to read the poem herself because he hadn't been man enough to reveal his shortcomings.

"Hey!"

Myles looked up at the sound of Ryan's familiar voice to find Brant and Levi approaching alongside him, tool belts around their waists. "You planning to do all of this yourself?" his youngest brother asked.

"Hernandez is coming," he answered.

The Wylder men looked at each other.

"I'll grab the coffee Mom sent." Brant returned to the truck parked on the street, out of the way. He returned with two thermoses and several metal cups. "All right, give us the list of things to tackle. I saw your sketches so I know there's lots."

"But what about chores?" Myles had begged favors from his brothers to cover for him today.

"Done," Ryan said.

Myles checked his watch. It was seven o'clock. Ryan normally wasn't even out at the ranch by now, and they were already finished? He smiled. For all the grief they gave you, brothers really were the best when you found yourself in a pinch.

"Let's start with fixing the roof, since we'll be tossing stuff down into the area we'll be focusing on next," he suggested.

A few hours later they were done with the roof and tackling details on the building's front. Apart from the absence of Cole, working together reminded Myles of when they'd built Brant's apartment above his veterinary clinic. It was seamless, often wordless laboring like they'd been doing it all their lives. Because they had.

"Did Cole ever pick up your call?" Myles asked Levi at one point, knowing he'd been trying to reach their missing brother.

Levi shook his head. The unspoken agreement was that if, by Levi's deadline, they couldn't get hold of him to see if he wanted his share of the ranch, they would all go looking for him. Myles really hoped Cole returned to Sweetheart Creek of his own volition.

As they hammered and sawed Myles caught Brant giving him a thoughtful look from time to time.

"What?" he finally asked him.

Brant cleared his throat. "How's that course going?" He was careful to look away, focus on his current task, and Myles hated that his brother felt he had to pussyfoot around the subject of him taking an online football coaching course.

"Fine." He was behind. Not completely sure he was going to pass, because every time he picked up the textbook and tried to read he'd hear the words in Karen's voice and have to put it down again.

Had Daisy-Mae been right about that author at yesterday's

party having the same reading issue he had? How had he made things work for him in a career that was all about reading, writing and messing about with the written word?

"You're taking a course?" Levi asked.

"Yup."

"In what? Cake decorating?" Ryan asked.

"No, that was Karen," Brant said. "She took it with Jackie and April over in Riverbend last spring."

Ryan sent Brant a dry look.

"Football," Myles stated.

"Football?" Ryan turned to him, his interest piqued. "The next level in coaching certification? The one you talked about?" He sounded excited, even though it would mean Myles would match his certification if he leveled up. "Is that where your idea about a backup for Hernandez came from? Because I am seriously loving having so many quarterback options right now."

"No. I'm only a few chapters in. Still stuck in the philosophy section." The philosophy of coaching. A sure way to make him want to give up on the course. They should start with the action. The good stuff. The nitty-gritty player-development tips. Then he'd be hooked even if the headaches started, unable to give up because the information he wanted would be right there, waiting for him to unearth it in that stew of mixed-up letters.

Or so he told himself.

His brothers were silent for a moment.

"Need help with it?" Levi asked.

"You going to read the book to me?"

Levi was watching him as though he might just do that.

"I'll borrow that reader-pen gadget from school," Ryan said.

"I don't need a pen."

"You run it over the lines of text and it reads them out loud."

"Seriously?" That might be exactly what he needed, and worth trying out. "That would be great, thanks."

"We just have to make sure we charge the battery and return it each morning or Mrs. Flatter will flip her lid."

"Deal."

They continued to work in silence again.

"Could that back stable at the ranch be added onto?" Ryan asked Levi a while later.

"What? Why?"

"To house more horses."

"Why would we want more horses?"

"We run a ranch, don't we?"

"Speaking of ranches, what's your decision about your share?" Levi leaned on the shovel he'd been using to remove dead shrubs from in front of the library where new flower boxes would go.

"I haven't decided," Ryan said. He turned to Brant. "Hey, so what are the bylaws on loose goats?"

Myles groaned. "Not this again."

"Yeah, this again. I found the new neighbor's goats eating the rosebush Mom and Laura just planted. Something has to be done."

Brant gave Myles a pointed look, then said casually to Ryan, "You should go talk to the new neighbor."

"I'd rather send you and your animal control badge after them so they get the message to lock up their goats."

"Brant's right," Myles said, leaning against the library wall. He figured Brant was up to something with Ryan, and he could serve as his wingman and help out. "You should chat with them first. Maybe they just need help fixing a gate. You're good at that stuff. And it's not like living next to us is always easy."

"There was that stampede we had last month," Levi said with a twist of his lips, as though trying not to smile.

"That was different. That was a one-time oops. This isn't," Ryan said.

"Talk to the neighbor," Brant urged once again.

"Have you given the neighbor a dog?" Ryan asked suspiciously, twigging on to the fact that there might be something behind his insistence on him going over to talk.

Brant laughed and returned to shoveling. "No."

At least not yet, he hadn't, judging from the gleam in his eyes, Myles figured. What was going on? And who was the new neighbor?

"Then maybe I *will* go have a talk," Ryan said carefully, still watching Brant.

"He gave Jackie a dog," Myles said. "And she's still single, you know."

Ryan scowled. "Tell her to take herself to a football game and find someone."

Myles laughed. He didn't think it worked that way, and his amusement faded as his mind drifted to Karen. They were both at football games all the time. Maybe they needed some of Jackie's matchmaking magic to get them back together again, because he sure did miss her, and he had no idea if her heart would ever open to him again.

Probably not.

"Karen's adopting Ribbons," Brant said, as though sensing where Myles's thoughts had gone.

He felt the weight of his brothers' gazes as he got back into his task of carefully painting the window trim. Too bad a dog didn't guarantee a mended heart.

Not long after the conversation died, Blake Hernandez, a young man willing to do anything to keep him and his loved one together, pulled up. Watching him smile and set to work, Myles finally realized exactly what he needed to do to win back Karen's heart.

ON MONDAY MORNING, in anticipation of the grand staying-open ceremony scheduled to be held in the library's parking lot, Karen left her car around the corner and collected her stack of thank-you cards for everyone who'd helped make the fundraiser a success.

She'd talked to her mom on the phone yesterday, and her silence, when she'd retold the story about the poetry reading onstage, had shamed her. The problem was, how could Myles ever forgive her for what she'd done when she had no plans to forgive herself?

She hadn't earned his trust and that had been the worst part. She missed him. And not just his kisses. He had given her permission to laugh loudly and be silly. To follow her heart and dream bigger in all areas of her life.

As Karen rounded the corner to the small parking area in front of the library, she nearly dropped her stack of thank-you cards.

The library was beautiful. It no longer looked rundown, but instead had a welcoming charm that could draw in even a crusty old codger like Henry.

She had known Myles was going to start the facelift yesterday, but she hadn't been prepared for this. He'd taken a budget of less than a thousand dollars and completely transformed the building.

Just like he'd transformed her.

She bit her bottom lip and sniffed.

"Well, don't blubber," Henry said, coming up beside her. "It's still just a building that might get closed up next year."

She reached for the board chairman with her free arm, pulling him into a hug. "Henry, it's so wonderful!"

He let her hold him for a second, before saying, "You're dripping on me. Your eyes are leaking, you silly woman."

"I'm just happy. Don't you ever cry from happiness?"

He adjusted the lapels of his light jacket. "I do my best not to."

"You should try it sometime."

He harrumphed and headed toward the building, then waited

to hold the door for her even though she moved slowly, taking in all the changes.

"There are flowers!" she said, as she moved past the freshly planted beds and boxes.

"And they will need watering."

She nodded. The building had been renewed, giving her hope. So much love had gone into this place, and she hoped that the man who'd done it all had some left over to sprinkle her way.

"There are shutters!"

"And they'll need to be painted every few years. Just like the trim."

When she got inside the building, she noticed a dog bed on the floor beside the circulation desk. She slowly turned to Henry, barely daring to ask.

He gave his classic frown and grumbled, "Ask Maria."

Today was shaping up to be a very good day. Karen just hoped she had the courage to pull off her plan to apologize to Myles. Publicly.

She had emailed him an invitation, like she had to everyone who had helped, but she hadn't received a reply. She began her morning duties, checking the book drop for returned items and signing them in. Her heart fell when, halfway through the stack, she came to an illustrated copy of *The Da Vinci Code.* There was no library stamp or bar code. It was the book she had given Myles.

She slowly turned it over, noticing a piece of paper peeking out. She shut her eyes, inhaling to bolster her courage, then slid the note from between the pages with a sigh.

Save a spot in today's ceremony for me. Two minutes tops.

The note was scrawled, barely legible. It wasn't signed, but she knew who it was from.

Her heart raced as she tried to decipher what Myles might have planned.

Realizing she had less than an hour until the ceremony began,

Karen hurried to the back room and collected a stack of chairs to put out for those who would tire from standing too long.

When she returned to the front of the library, Brant was there with Ribbons, holding her leash and smiling. "I hereby congratulate you on your adoption of Ribbons, as well as her newly appointed status as the Sweetheart Creek Library mascot and service animal," he declared.

Karen gasped and crouched to pet the freshly groomed dog. "Thank you!" She fingered the ribbons in the dog's tufts of fur. "She's gorgeous."

"I figured I could present her during the ceremony, if that works."

"Beautifully. Oh, I'm so happy."

"And I'm happy your cats don't mind, and that the board said yes."

"Me, too." As far as Karen could tell, everything was coming together this morning. She just hoped the universe had room in its schedule for one more good thing.

If so, all she needed was for Myles to show up.

And forgive her.

Before she could allow herself to begin fretting over all the holes in her plan, Brant asked, lowering his voice as he craned his neck looking for his great-uncle, "How'd you get the Ribbons idea past Henry?"

"The bylaws didn't specify anything about animals."

"I love loopholes."

"And really, he's not that bad." She lowered her voice as well. "He let me hug him today."

"Did he combust?"

"Well, come to think of it, I haven't seen him lately, and there has been the odd burning scent that I've caught here and there…"

Brant grinned and helped her carry out chairs. Soon the parking lot was filled with people gathering for the ceremony and board members serving punch and cookies. Someone had found a long red ribbon they strung across the main doorway, waiting to be cut.

Davis Davies, the Sweetheart Creek DJ, had his station wagon in the parking lot, with equipment and cords strung about as he prepared to broadcast the ceremony on the radio. Though the idea made Karen nervous, she reminded herself that only about a thousand people tuned in to the local station, and those who cared most would be present to hear it live, anyway.

She stood off to the side with Brant and Ribbons while board members opened the ceremony. Brant was called on to announce Ribbons as a new honorary member, amidst cheers. Then Henry began discussing the various donations made and fundraising efforts done within the past few weeks. He was impressively civil and complimentary. He almost sounded as if he wanted the library to stay open.

"I now turn this over to the woman who made it all possible through her own initiative. Thanks to Karen Hartley, you have a community library for at least another ten months."

Drawing a deep breath, Karen stepped up to the microphone and fervently thanked everyone from those who'd brought their wares to the fair's market, to those who'd been on the rodeo grounds late into the night to set up the fair. To prize donors and volunteers, to the caterer and band, and to everyone who'd attended and even to those who'd knocked Myles into the dunk tank. The audience was smiling, amused. She'd thanked everyone and couldn't draw it out any longer, but she still didn't see Myles anywhere, and the next part of her speech was for him.

"Myles Wylder," she said, her voice wavering, "challenged me to dream bigger." She gestured to the building behind her, hoping he was at least listening to her on the radio. "I was afraid to fail, and worried that I would look foolish if I did. I was afraid to come up with ideas bigger than a bake sale, and he gave me a mental shake up."

She paused briefly and several people in the audience smiled, likely understanding just how much a man like Myles had changed her quiet, rule-abiding life.

"I admire how he stood up for something he believed in, dedicating time and money even though this isn't a place where he spends the majority of his time." She paused again to let that sink in, then hurried on before the ache in her chest caused her eyes to well up with tears and her voice to quaver. "He is a true community member. Like many of you, he gives everything he has because this town matters to him. I don't see him here today, but I hope he knows that I love everything he did for us with this project. Everything from daring me to dream bigger, to encouraging me to step outside my comfort zone, to getting me to climb onto that crazy trampoline of Daisy-Mae's." She fingered the top button of her blouse while she waited for the chatter about the popular trampoline to subside.

"And I want to thank him for supporting me in taking life by the horns. We became very close during those two crazy weeks of planning and I believed I knew him. But because I acted on assumption after assumption, I didn't earn the trust I should have, and I ended up blindly doing something horribly humiliating to a man I care deeply about."

She forced herself to look out at the crowd, receiving a thumbs-up from Jackie and a supportive smile from Jenny, who was standing beside her. "I was afraid of losing the library two weeks ago. And as awful and selfish as it sounds, I wish I had, because what I lost, and what I did, was so much worse. I lost something irreplaceable."

She caught a glimpse of Maria in the front row, inhaling as though bracing herself for this awkward confession. Karen looked away in shame.

"I've learned a lot about myself in the past two weeks. I already knew that I'm a book snob. I love books. I love everything about them, from the way they smell to how they feel, to the perfection of a brand new book to the crisp font of a black-

and-white ereader. And even how fast I can blow through a hundred dollars in a bookstore." She slowed her words, tempered her enthusiasm. "But what I learned is that my snobbery is uncalled for. I used it as a shield to disregard people who don't share that interest—or what I feebly called passion. It allowed me to justify making dismissive assumptions about others, and to build a case of either you are with me as a book nerd or somehow apart from me, and therefore to be excluded from my inner circle, because how could we ever have anything in common? The worst part is that I made an assumption about Myles. As a result I put him in a position I..."

She looked up again as a large figure marched into her periphery. It was Myles, his expression unreadable. Karen staggered back, away from the microphone.

"I learned a lot working with Karen," he said, smoothly taking the microphone from its stand and holding it in his hand, his back to her.

"I'm doing something here, right now," Karen said uncertainly.

"I know, and I appreciate that." Myles glanced back at her. Her breathing hiccuped in her chest as he gave her a soft look meant to blunt the hurt of his abrupt dismissal.

He turned back to the crowd. "I'm dyslexic."

Karen put her fingers to her lips, afraid that she'd somehow pushed him to speak publicly about something he didn't ever talk about.

"But I'm not stupid," he said gently, yet firmly, addressing the crowd.

"I know that," she said, as their audience shifted uneasily. Karen took a half step forward, horrified at how Myles was baring everything—because of her and her thoughtlessness. "Nobody thinks that."

"Karen called me on that in a way nobody else ever has. She's fearless in her assumptions." Myles put an arm around her shoulders, drawing her up beside him. "It's one of the things I love most about her."

She shook her head. "That's not my best trait," she whispered.

"She assumed I'm a good reader. You know why she assumed that? Because I lied to her."

A murmur ran through the gathering, like a light breeze blowing through the parking lot.

"She assumed I'm a great reader because I can talk a good game about *The Da Vinci Code*, thanks to Ryan." He pointed to his brother in the crowd. "I also write a pretty kick-butt poem, thanks to Brant's typing skills and his ability to spell and put letters down in the correct order." He gestured again and Brant blinked back at him, his mouth set in a firm line.

"I also took Karen to a place where poets and songwriters hang out." He paused for a half beat, looking at her, snug under his arm. "I played a pretty good game, didn't I?"

She nodded, realizing that neither of them had behaved perfectly, and that both of them had remained hidden behind their fears.

"Karen assumed I love books as much as she does because I wanted her to. Just like I wanted everyone in town to assume I was a harmless jock who just didn't read much. Because it was safer. But Karen also assumed other things. Things I didn't manipulate. She assumed I was worth trusting with a crazy-big library plan so she wouldn't have to leave her community and pursue her book fetishes elsewhere." He smiled at her and was rewarded with laughter, from her and the crowd.

"Karen Hartley is the one my grandmother Ruth Wylder told me to wait for when I was in high school and lamenting my lot in life. She told me to stop dating women who didn't challenge me, or who let me stay in that safe zone that didn't make me live up to my potential. She assured me that if I waited, the right woman would come along. A woman who saw me for who I really am." Myles was quiet for a moment, his head bowed. Then he shifted to face Karen, his eyes sad. "Is it any wonder that when I found her I didn't want to risk losing her by telling her I wasn't a book nerd? That I can't even read properly?"

Karen placed her hands on either side of his face, with tears streaming down her own. "I am so sorry I wasn't worthy of your trust."

"I didn't trust myself, Kitty."

The tears flowed harder as she realized that everything was going to be okay. They were going to forgive each other and themselves and move past this. Together.

"You know," she said carefully, "if you still have that bracelet of your grandma's I'd probably wear it." As she spoke she realized she'd last seen it on Daisy-Mae. "Or whatever. Maybe just take me out for coffee sometime."

"If I had that bracelet would you accept it?"

"I might not give it back this time."

"Is that a promise?"

"Pretty sure it's a threat."

Eyes twinkling with happiness, Myles swept her into his arms and kissed her thoroughly, earning a very loud round of applause, along with a bark of approval from Ribbons.

"Are we done here?" Henry grumbled, stepping forward. He tried to pry the microphone from Myles.

"No," he and Karen said at the same time.

"We are only just beginning," she murmured, still in Myles's arms.

Myles flashed that handsome Wylder grin and confessed into the microphone, "I love Karen Hartley."

Karen laughed, happier than she'd ever been, and not at all embarrassed that their proclamations of love as well as their fears and flaws had been broadcast across the county thanks to Sweetheart Creek's radio station.

"I love you, too, Myles. And always will."

EPILOGUE

$\mathcal{M}$yles sat in the Sweet Meadows Ranch kitchen a week before Thanksgiving, hours after the football team had won area playoffs, sending them even closer to the state championship game, which would be held just before Christmas in Dallas.

The Torpedoes were real contenders for the trophy, as they had been for the past several years, and Hernandez had played his best game of the season tonight. But Myles was worried. Karen had called him two hours ago, panicked that Blake's girlfriend, Robyn, had come home from the game to find herself kicked out of the house. Robyn had called Karen; Karen had called Myles. Myles had called his family.

This wasn't just a personal crisis for Robyn, but something with potentially large ripple effects. It could jeopardize the way Blake played, which might then impact the team, and their playoff games. That could put scholarships at risk, seriously effecting Blake and Robyn's future. So many things hinged on the young couple remaining in a good headspace over the next few weeks, so Myles and Karen had gathered the Wylder clan around the kitchen table in the old ranch house. Myles's mom was at the counter, whipping up a midnight snack for the group.

"Robyn's sleeping on my couch tonight, but she needs somewhere more permanent to go," Karen said, and Myles squeezed her hand.

"That poor girl," Maria said with a tsking sound. "That's the last thing she needs. Pregnant, and now no support from her family."

"Blake's family is living in close quarters right now," Karen explained. "They're having asbestos removed and it's probably not the best place for a pregnant woman in any case. And it sounds like money is really tight. They weren't expecting this renovation expense. Add in a baby…"

"When is she due?" Brant asked.

"Just before summer break."

"Is she going to stay in school?" Laura asked.

"She'd like to, and I think it's important that she does." Myles snugged his chair close to Karen's and slid an arm around her shoulders. She leaned into him with a smile that warmed his heart.

"I've already talked to the principal to see what we can do to modify her program so she can graduate with her class," Ryan said. "We'll get her her diploma."

"I can move back here," Brant said. "She can stay in my apartment above the vet clinic."

"She can't afford rent," Myles said.

"You think I'd charge her?" His brother appeared mildly insulted.

"She's not looking for handouts," Karen said. "She wants to stand on her own two feet, not feel underfoot at a friend's or at Blake's."

"She could walk the dogs or clean the office to feel as though she's contributing something, right, Brant?" Maria suggested.

"Of course. And she can stay as long as y'all don't mind me living here."

"It's your home, too," Levi said.

"You should take your house back," Laura told Brant. "I can find somewhere else." He'd bought her great-aunt's home from her last month and had been renting it to her after she'd returned to Sweetheart Creek to be close to Levi.

"Not necessary." Brant shook his head. "I can move into my old bedroom here. There's no need to uproot you."

"Unless Laura wants to move in here?" Levi watched his girl-friend closely. Her cheeks grew pink as she considered the offer.

"No way," Myles said, removing his arm from around Karen's shoulders and straightening his spine. "I don't want to feel like a third wheel in my own home."

"Oh, it's yours now?" Ryan asked drily.

"I live here. Do you?"

"No, but I still own as much of it as you do."

"Yeah, and thanks for fixing the doors like I asked you to," Levi retorted.

"I noticed they were closing better," Ryan said.

"That's because *I* fixed them." Levi frowned at him.

"I'm not ready to live with Levi," Laura said, raising her voice slightly in order to end the bickering between the brothers. "But thank you."

"Robyn's going to need money for baby things, food and maternity clothes," Brant interjected.

"She's already covered for maternity wear," Karen said, checking a list she'd made at some point in the evening. "There's a group of moms that have a big bin of clothes they pass around to whoever is pregnant. It's already in my car."

Myles smiled at her, loving that she was just as willing to step in and help as his family and the community were. This, right here, was what Sweetheart Creek was all about.

"Blake's working part-time at the hardware store and should be able to help her with some expenses," Ryan said.

"I'll keep tutoring him," Karen said. "Help him stay focused on his grades."

For the next several minutes they worked out other items Robyn and Blake might need over the next few months, resolving the issue as best as they could for the night. At last Karen claimed with a yawn that it was time for her to go home.

"Hey," Myles said, tugging her close for a goodbye kiss on the front porch a few minutes later.

She leaned against him, saying, "I never want to leave this town."

"Good. Me either." He walked her to her car. "Thanks for what you're doing for Robyn. And Blake, too. It'll help him focus on football."

"It's always about football, isn't it?" Karen teased.

"In this case, yeah. I hope he can get some scholarships, and I hope the sport takes the two of them good places. They deserve a shot."

"I was joking, Myles," Karen said, snuggling in against him. Her blouse was still done up to her chin, but he didn't mind. To him, that was Karen.

"I'm glad you Wylder guys are helping these kids," she said. "It's very paternal of you, cowboy."

He let out a soft huff of amusement. "Then you're maternal, Madam Librarian. And just so you know, us cowboys take care of our own." He pulled her into a long kiss, sliding his hand under the hem of her jacket to press against her lower back. During the next kiss he twisted the material of her blouse from the waistband of her pants and placed his palm there, skin on her skin. The kiss deepened until he heard the ranch door close and footsteps pad across the porch and down the steps.

Ryan. His brother stepped off the path, walking through the

grass to his Jeep. Myles gave Karen another kiss, ignoring him until he cursed.

"Those goats!" Ryan yelled.

"What's going on?" called Maria, leaning out the front door.

"Those goats are using our lawn like a litter box."

"I think it's time for me to leave," Karen said with a small smile.

Myles caught her hand. "Are you doing anything tomorrow?"

"We have cheer practice in the morning. And it sounds like I'm helping Robyn move into Brant's apartment."

"Right. That. Is Robyn going to practice?"

"She plans to keep coming to support the other girls."

"Okay. Well, we'll move Brant out in the morning and then hopefully get her in by the afternoon, and then the rest of the day is ours. How does that sound?"

"Amazing." She rose up onto her tiptoes to kiss his chin.

He pulled her into a hug. "Have I ever told you that I love you?"

She smiled up at him. "I can't remember. Maybe you'd better tell me again."

"I love you. I'm glad my grandma was right, and that I waited, and that I finally found you."

"Who knew I would develop a thing for cowboys, and that cowboys play golf?"

"Cowboys make the best boyfriends, you know."

"That's what I like about you. You're so modest." She laughed, sliding out of his arms before he could tickle her in retaliation for her comment.

"I'm going to go over there," Ryan announced, "and tell that Clarke fellow to keep his goats on his own property."

Levi smirked from his spot on the porch, where he and Laura were saying their own good-nights. "I would love for you to do that." His expression grew thoughtful. "But maybe not at one in the morning."

Karen groaned. "My wake-up alarm is going to go off way too soon."

Myles held her car door for her, stealing another kiss. "It won't come soon enough for me."

She grasped his shirtfront, kissing him again, and he shivered, not from the midnight chill, but from the intensity of the kiss. "You know," she murmured, "I've been wondering. Did you really write that poem for me?"

"Yes!"

"I thought so. But I'm trying this new thing called not assuming. Turns out it's pretty difficult."

"Brant typed it up because sometimes I put down the wrong words. It's just easier if he's my scribe."

"He doesn't mind?"

Myles smiled. "Sometimes."

"Let him know I'm expecting more poetry on Valentine's Day and to warm up his typing fingers."

"You want to wait that long?"

Karen laughed. "No, but I don't want to make assumptions."

"I like it when you do."

"Such as?"

"Such as when you assume that we're going on a date tomorrow night."

"Did I make an assumption about that?"

"I think we should assume that every Saturday night from now on you'll be busy with me."

"I think I like that idea, Myles Cameron Wylder."

He grinned. "I love it when you call me that."

"And I love you." She smiled and closed her car door, then drove out to the gravel road that would take her toward town.

Myles couldn't wait for tomorrow.

Ryan Wylder

RYAN CLAPPED his hands at the neighbor's goats as they nibbled their way through the front garden. One turned to look at him.

"Come on, Lupe. Round up these goats. Let's take 'em home." He tried to emulate the hand signals he'd seen Levi give the Australian shepherd when it was roundup time.

"You can't be serious. The neighbors will be sleeping," Levi stated.

"I saw lights on when I arrived earlier," Laura said.

"That was at least an hour ago," Levi argued.

"Done deal," Ryan said, grateful to have Laura on his side. He might feel helpless when it came to their top quarterback and his life predicament, but this was something he could take care of. Right now. "Come on, Lupe. Let's go."

Levi sighed and gave Lupe the signal, sending the dog into action. "I don't think this is a good idea."

"Why not?"

His brother hesitated. "Nobody likes being confronted by an irate neighbor in the middle of the night. And they could be asleep by now."

"Fine. I'll just put these guys in their pen and come back home. Maybe put a padlock on the damn thing. Or tie them up in Clarke's flower garden. See how he likes that."

This was at least the fourth time the goats had shown up on the Wylder ranch. It was time to go talk to that guy, middle of the night or not.

Coaxing Levi's dog to herd the goats toward the neighboring ranch, Ryan passed Carmichael's place, the original homestead, and saw that a light was still on inside. What was his grandfather doing up at this time of night? Did nobody sleep at a reasonable hour anymore?

Once on the neighbor's property, Ryan was glad for the light of a full moon. He wasn't quite as familiar with the lay of the land, even though he'd spent many hours trekking over here as a kid to enjoy fresh baked cookies from the previous owner.

About five minutes later, the old ranch house came into view, a sprawling Spanish-style dwelling with a clay-tile roof and stuccoed mud walls that would keep the place cool during the hottest Texan days. The yard was looking overgrown, the house a bit run down. Rumor had it the new owner had come from the city. And, based on what Ryan had observed so far, obviously didn't know a thing about ranch life.

"Your goats are out!" he hollered as he wandered behind the house, recalling there used to be several corrals to the left. Under a yard light about fifty feet away from the house, he found a small one that looked like it had been used recently and should keep goats in. After herding the animals to the property line, Lupe had refused to go farther, but by then the goats had seemed happy enough to return home. They headed toward the corral, then stopped several feet short of the gate and looked at Ryan. He went around behind them to herd them into the open pen and stepped in fresh droppings in the process.

Seriously? These were his good sneakers from coaching, not his cowboy boots, which shucked crap off them like a frozen puck down clear ice.

"In! Get in there!" he yelled at the goats. Then for good measure, hollered in the direction of the house, "Take care of your damn goats!"

He heard the telltale *click, click* of a shotgun sending a bullet into its chamber, and one of the goats let out a baying sound. Ryan raised his hands in the air, slowly turning. He kept his anger in check and said evenly, "Your goats were in our yard again. I think it's time you learned how to secure them, as the damages are starting to add up."

He peered at the neighbor, but instead of seeing a man found himself facing a woman, one with lovely dark brown skin. A woman wearing a white nightgown and pointing a shotgun at his chest. Her head was tilted, her right eye sighting the weapon, her stance wide, her hands steady.

It was the gorgeous woman with the wedding band from the fundraiser dance, and she meant business. The way she handled the gun said she was comfortable with its power to change lives. He had a suspicion she'd spent some time training in the Army Reserves like he and his brothers had, or else had grown up hunting.

The yard light cast a glow through her nightgown, and Ryan, his hands still in the air, found himself admiring her curves. She was stunning, from the serious dark eyes, the unruly mess of black curls, the skin that created its own shadows, to the feet hastily shoved into brown cowboy boots. He liked a woman who took care of her own business, even if that business was him.

But then, if she did take care of business, why were these goats continually roaming the Sweet Meadows Ranch? Something didn't add up.

Where was Clarke, anyway? And why was he letting his wife take on an intruder? She was the wife, right?

Ryan licked his lips, settling on something to say.

"I'm Ryan Wylder, from next door. Well, I live in town, but I'm part owner of the Sweet Meadows Ranch." He couldn't seem to draw his gaze from the curves of her waist and hips. She was all woman.

He slowly lowered his hands, his earlier annoyance over the goats forgotten. "I can see through your nightgown."

Wordlessly, the woman aimed her weapon to the sky and fired. Ryan ducked instinctively, cupping his ears as darkness took over once again, the pale moonlight leaving him at a disadvantage in a yard he didn't know.

He dared a glance at the yard light. She had blown the bulb to pieces.

"Nice shot."

"Thank you for returning my goats." The gun was slung across her chest now, her stance at ease, but he knew she was ready to fire again at a moment's notice if need be. "Now get off my property."

Ryan straightened slowly, considering the woman. "Who are you?"

"You, a lewd voyeur peeping through my nightgown—"

"It's not my fault you have an appealing choice in nightwear."

"—want to have a conversation with a woman holding a loaded shotgun?" Her anger had returned.

"You haven't reloaded the chamber, so I figured it would be a good time to discuss the weather, and how the creek that runs through both our properties is subject to flash floods every once in a while." He shivered at a long-ago memory of being washed away, helpless in the current after listening to his brothers talk about where to step in order to stay safe. "Maybe chat about how Clarke—your husband?—can't seem to keep your goats in a pen."

Her shoulders dropped in frustration. "One of them is an escape artist. I apologize if they've been a nuisance."

"A nuisance? I'll say!" He scanned the herd. "This one! This one with the white goatee?" He gave an indignant huff. "He bit me. In the butt."

He saw the woman suck in her cheeks and her eyebrows crashed down.

"It's not funny!" he said. "And I don't appreciate being shot at."

"I don't appreciate you trespassing in the middle of the night and then gawking at me!" The gun was lifting again, his hands following its movement upward.

"Point taken."

"Good, because those lights are expensive and changing the bulb is going to be a real pain in the backside."

Ryan's phone rang and he ignored it. Then he thought better of it. It was his mother's ring tone, and she had no doubt heard the gunshot. She was probably wondering if she needed to come over with her first-aid kit to throw a little dirt in a bullet hole and tell him to buck up and carry on.

Ryan held up a finger, then slowly took his phone from his back pocket. "I should probably get this."

The woman shifted uneasily, and he explained, "It's my mother."

He held the phone to his ear and Maria immediately asked, "You okay? I heard a shot."

"Hey, Mom. Just meeting the neighbors—*neighbor*."

"Don't come home with any extra holes in you," she said sternly.

"I won't." As he put the phone back in his pocket, he noticed a trembling in his hands. He inhaled slowly, knowing the adrenaline wouldn't last.

"It's the middle of the night," the woman announced.

She had come closer and he realized he didn't recognize her beyond seeing her at the dance.

"How have I not seen you around town?" he asked. "Do you live here? Are you just visiting?"

"Why haven't I seen you next door? I've met Myles, Levi, Brant, Maria and that old guy who eats candy at nine in the morning. It sounds like you're just a wannabe rancher clinging to their coattails."

"Me?" Trying to keep from exploding, he looked back at the house. "Where's Clarke? And who are you?"

"I'm Carly Clarke." She put out her hand, and he found her strong grip matching his. She squeezed, he squeezed. She stared at him in the moonlight and he stared right back.

Clarke was a last name. And Clarke had a wife. Carly. Beautiful Carly, who did the man's dirty work.

"Where's your husband? We need to talk about his goats."

"How old-fashioned of you, asking for the *man*," she growled.

Ryan swallowed hard. He liked to think of himself as someone who supported equality and all it entailed. But obviously, he had some room to grow. Just because most ranches were run by men around here didn't mean the women couldn't answer every single question anyone asked.

"Fine. They're your goats? Let's talk about the damage they've done to my mom's roses."

No wonder Levi had kept smirking whenever Ryan referred to "Clarke's goats." He'd kept saying *his* goats and Levi had known better.

He wondered if the way the fight was going out of him after finding out they were her goats was patriarchal, too. Or maybe it was because she was gorgeous and he wanted a chance with her if she ever tossed the useless husband aside. Or maybe it was because he'd been raised to treat women kindly, not fight them with unrelenting determination.

Carly changed everything.

No, it changed nothing. Except she was beautiful and full of fire, in a way that intrigued him and made him want to move back to the ranch so he could be closer in order to figure her out.

What was wrong with him?

"I like how you shot out that light," he commented.

Her scowl deepened. "You need to get off my ranch."

Okay, so she wanted him to treat her like a man. No compliments or buttering up. Get down to business. Fight hard. He could do that.

Happily.

"You need to keep your goats on your property." The goateed butt-nibbler was edging around behind him and Ryan shifted, trying to act cool while also making sure his buttocks were safely outside the nipping zone.

"I'm working on it," Carly said coolly.

"Next time I see them over on our ranch, I'm going to feed them something that will spoil their milk. They're for milking, aren't they?"

Carly narrowed her eyes, the gun swinging idly in her right hand. "If you hurt my animals…"

"I won't. I'm a rancher. I'll just mess with your profits." As soon as he said that he regretted it. He was being a jerk. He couldn't treat her like he'd treat a dude. She'd take it too personally. There was something fierce about Carly, but something vulnerable, too.

"You don't want me as an enemy," she said, conviction in her tone.

"And you…" Ryan pulled in a breath, remembering Levi's warning about neighbors and getting along. Which he seemed to be pretty adept at *not* doing right now. "You can thank me for returning your goats any time you feel the need to do so."

"I already did."

"Funny, I'm pretty sure I would have recalled that."

"I didn't shoot you, did I?"

Ryan laughed, then bit it off when he found she wasn't laughing with him. They stared at each other for a long moment and he didn't know whether to despise her or ask her out on a date.

Then again, there was still that issue of the wedding band on her left hand.

"Where *is* your husband?" Was he out of town? AWOL? In the forces? Working on oil rigs? Sweetheart Creek wasn't a place to let something as exciting as a newcomer's arrival slip past the gossip gates without fanfare and speculation. He hadn't heard a whisper about her husband, which seemed odd, although he hadn't heard much about her, either. Then again, he had been pretty head-down and into football lately.

"Unless you're going to fix the pen," Carly said, her earlier bite returning, "it's time for you to go home."

"You know, since I'm already over here and we're both up…" He glanced at the shot-out light. "Although fixing a pen is usually easier when there's some light on the subject."

"Well, now who's to blame for that?"

She shifted the gun to rest in both hands and Ryan caught her quick smirk. He liked this woman. Even though there was something about her that didn't add up and threw him off balance. Or maybe that was *why* he liked her.

As he stood there trying to figure her out he couldn't help but feel a little bit as though he'd finally met his match.

THE COWBOY'S OF SWEETHEART CREEK, TEXAS

Read them all!

The Cowboy's Stolen Heart (Levi)

The Cowboy's Secret Wish (Myles)

The Cowboy's Second Chance (Ryan)

The Cowboy's Sweet Elopement (Brant)

The Cowboy's Surprise Return (Cole)

There are more Sweetheart Creek stories set in Indigo Bay! Maria has her own special story, Sweet Joymaker. Their cousin Nick's story is Sweet Troublemaker. And you can't forget about the Wylders' cousin Alexa! Her story is Sweet Holiday Surprise.

Indigo Bay

Sweet romances set in a beach town—meet characters new and old in this spinoff series.

Sweet Matchmaker (Ginger and Logan)

Sweet Holiday Surprise (Cash & Alexa)

Sweet Forgiveness (Ashton & Zoe)

Sweet Troublemaker (Nick & Polly)

Sweet Joymaker (Maria & Clint)

VEILS AND VOWS

Find love in unexpected places with these sweet marriage of convenience romances.

The Promise (Book 0: Devon & Olivia)

The Surprise Wedding (Book 1: Devon & Olivia)

A Pinch of Commitment (Book 2: Ethan & Lily)

The Wedding Plan (Book 3: Luke & Emma)

Accidentally Married (Book 4: Burke & Jill)

The Marriage Pledge (Book 5: Moe & Amy)

Mail Order Soulmate (Book 6: Zach & Catherine)

THE SUMMER SISTERS

Taming billionaires has never been so *sweet*.

Falling for billionaires has never been so sweet.

* Available in paperback & ebook & audio! *

One cottage. Four sisters. And four billionaires who will sweep them off their feet.

Falling for the Movie Star

Falling for the Boss

Falling for the Single Dad

Falling for the Bodyguard

Falling for the Firefighter

ABOUT THE AUTHOR

Jean Oram is a *New York Times* and *USA Today* bestselling romance author. Inspiration for her small town series came from her own upbringing on the Canadian prairies. Although, so far, none of her characters have grown up in an old schoolhouse or worked on a bee farm. Jean still lives on the prairie with her husband, two kids, and big shaggy dog where she can be found out playing in the snow or hiking.

Become an Official Fan:
www.facebook.com/groups/jeanoramfans
Newsletter: www.jeanoram.com/FREEBOOK
Twitter: www.twitter.com/jeanoram
Instagram: www.instagram.com/author_jeanoram
Facebook: www.facebook.com/JeanOramAuthor
Website & blog: www.jeanoram.com

CPSIA information can be obtained
at www.ICGtesting.com
Printed in the USA
LVHW031255221220
674885LV00006B/299